Her Suffering

Copyright © 2017 Jon Athan
All Rights Reserved.

This is a work of fiction. Names, characters, businesses, places, events and incidents are either the products of the author's imagination or used in a fictitious manner. Any resemblance to actual persons, living or dead, or actual events is purely coincidental.

For more information on this book or the author, please visit www.jon-athan.com. General inquiries are welcome.

Facebook:
https://www.facebook.com/AuthorJonAthan
Twitter: @Jonny_Athan
Email: info@jon-athan.com

Book cover by Sig: http://inkubusdesign.com/

Thank you for the support!

ISBN: 9798637022588

First Edition

WARNING

This book contains scenes of intense violence and some disturbing themes. Some parts of this book may be considered violent, cruel, disturbing, or unusual. Certain implications may also trigger strong emotional responses. This book is *not* intended for those easily offended or appalled. Please enjoy at your own discretion.

Table of Contents

Chapter One 1
Chapter Two 15
Chapter Three 21
Chapter Four 33
Chapter Five 43
Chapter Six 51
Chapter Seven 63
Chapter Eight 69
Chapter Nine 79
Chapter Ten 89
Chapter Eleven 101
Chapter Twelve 113
Chapter Thirteen 121
Chapter Fourteen 129
Chapter Fifteen 145
Chapter Sixteen 153
Chapter Seventeen 159
Chapter Eighteen 173
Chapter Nineteen 181
Chapter Twenty 201

Chapter One

When It Began

"I should be going inside," Julie Knight said, her voice tender and comforting.

The eighteen-year-old woman sat in the passenger seat of a little red hatchback. From her seat, she could see her single-story home down the street. Light poured out of the windows and illuminated the night—calling to her. She shuffled in her seat, calm but uncomfortable, and turned towards her boyfriend—*Daniel Harris.*

Daniel paid her no mind, though. The handsome young man—twenty-one years old, to be exact—was too busy fiddling with his glass marijuana pipe. He carefully packed the bowl, licking his lips like a starved man at a buffet. He lit the bowl and took a puff. He chuckled as he coughed, then he held the pipe up to Julie's chest.

With a deadpan expression, Julie repeated, "I should be going inside."

"Come on. Take a hit, babe. Just one," Daniel said, a devilish smirk on his face. "*Come on,* a little bud never hurt anyone."

"My mom will smell it, Daniel. She has the nose of a damn K-9. You know that already."

"Yeah, yeah... I guess you're right. With a nose like that, she could probably work as a police dog for a living, huh? Wait a second, you said she was looking for a new job, right? I think I have an idea."

Julie playfully slapped Daniel's arm and giggled, amused by the joke. Daniel chuckled, then he took another hit from the pipe. Julie's smile vanished as she watched her boyfriend. She wasn't disappointed in him, though. His joke led her to a maze of doubt where one question reigned supreme: *what am I doing with my life?*

She asked, "How's your job hunt going?"

As plumes of smoke danced out of his mouth, undulating towards the ceiling of the car, Daniel responded, "Job hunt? I think it's going... *good.* We've talked about this, babe. I don't really want a... a 'traditional' job. I'm looking for an independent career. You know, something where *I'm* the boss of *me.* It's coming together. Don't worry about that..." He glanced over at his girlfriend, still smirking. In a condescending tone, he asked, "How's 'saving for college' going?"

"Fine. *Dandy.* Thirty percent of my check from the diner goes to my savings and the rest pays some bills, which means I can't really buy shit for myself, but it's fine. It's going to be worth it, Daniel. You can keep talking shit, but I know it's going to be worth it."

She crossed her arms and turned in her seat, flustered. She stared at the dashboard as she thought about Daniel and her future—the pair didn't mix well. She wouldn't admit it to him, but she didn't picture him as part of her successful future. It hurt her to think about it. Yet, the thoughts became stronger as Daniel continued to ridicule her dreams and goals.

Daniel said, "It'll work out, babe. I can be a successful entrepreneur and you can be a successful teacher or... or something. It's better than me doing all of the work while you spend all of my money. Actually, it might just be perfect if you went to school and became a teacher. I always wanted to date one. It's kinda hot, isn't it?"

He leaned closer to his girlfriend. He kissed her cheek, then he pecked her neck. He gently caressed her cheek as he nibbled on her neck. He moved up to her chin, then he kissed her lips. The kiss wasn't fueled by passion, but he couldn't tell the difference.

As soon as Daniel squeezed her breast, Julie pushed his hands away and leaned towards the door. Her boyfriend was obviously eager, but she wasn't interested.

She shook her head and said, "We're not doing this right now."

"Why not? It's, um... It's kinda kinky, isn't it? Banging in public?"

"No. I think it's kinda illegal. Besides, I live here. If I get caught, everyone is going to hear about it."

"So? We're just two young, naive adults having fun..."

Daniel fondled her breast and kissed her again.

Julie pushed him off her and sternly said, "I said 'no,' okay? No, no, *no*. I'm not in the mood."

Daniel returned to his seat. He sighed in disappointment, then he said, "We fuck, like, once a week, Julie. I mean, sometimes, we don't even mess around for *two* weeks. I have urges, you know?" He smiled and said, "I have needs, too."

"We do it whenever we have the chance. I go out of my way to have sex with you, even when I don't have time. I'm not some sex-machine, okay? I have feelings, too, and everything can't be fixed with sex. So, just chill with that. I'm tired and I'm not in the mood."

"I get it. Whatever, whatever..."

Julie crossed her arms again and turned her attention to the windshield. She stared at her house from afar, ready to head home.

Before she could say another word, Daniel asked, "You want to, um... to snort some coke?"

Julie shook her head and asked, "You're still messing with that shit?"

"It's good for business. You don't have to snort it, either. You can just rub it on your gums. Your mom won't notice a thing. Unless you go home and French kiss her or something..."

Julie sighed in disappointment. She was dating a drug dealer who got high on his own supply. He wasn't a bad man, he tried his best to please his girlfriend, but he was undoubtedly a disappointment. She couldn't muster the energy to argue with him.

She grabbed her bag and opened the door, then she said, "No, thanks." She hopped out of the car, then she leaned closer to the door. She said, "Be careful with all of that shit, Danny. Smoking is fine, a little coke on the side probably never killed anyone, but you know what they say: you shouldn't mix your vices. It'll mess with your heart and your head. Get home safe, okay? I love you."

As his girlfriend closed the door, Daniel said, "I love you, too, babe."

Julie briskly walked down the street, her white sneakers thudding on the cracked pavement. She strolled onto the sidewalk, clutching her bag close to her chest. Her long black hair danced with the cool breeze. Her white button-up shirt, which was tucked into her black skirt, rustled with each step.

The area wasn't affluent, but it wasn't bad, either.

She simply wanted to get home. She couldn't help but sigh in relief as she reached her house—the little blue house just beyond the short chain-link fence.

***

Julie wrestled with her keys as she stepped into the house. She muttered to herself about the busted lock, saying something along the lines of: *stupid thing, always getting stuck.* She pulled her key out, then she slammed the door. Frustrated, she approached the first archway to her left and gazed into the narrow kitchen. There was another archway leading into the living room in the kitchen, too.

She asked, "You finish eating already, squirt?"

Nick Knight, Julie's thirteen-year-old brother, stood near the sink and washed the dishes. His boredom was evident from the dull expression on his round face. He glanced back at the archway and nodded.

He said, "Yeah. We ate spaghetti. I think there's still some left if you want to serve yourself. I'm not washing your dishes, though."

"I wasn't going to make you wash them."

"Yeah, *right...*"

"Whatever. I'm not hungry anyway. See you around, squirt."

Julie stepped forward, then she stopped, the floorboards creaking under her shoes. She stared into the living room to her left.

Reina Knight, Julie's mother, sat on a sofa at the center of the living room. Hair tied in a bun and a blue bathrobe draped over her lean figure, the middle-aged woman shuffled through a stack of papers while constantly glancing at her cell phone. She occasionally muttered to herself about her finances—*when did I spend $20.45?*

Shoulders and heels raised, Julie tiptoed towards the hallway to her right. She wasn't in the mood for talking. She certainly didn't want to talk about her boring day.

Without glancing back, Reina said, "Julie, don't go to your room without talking to me."

Julie lowered her shoulders and head. She spun in place, then she leaned on the wall and stared at her mother.

Julie asked, "What's up, mom?"

Flicking her finger across her phone, Reina asked, "How's work been treating you, sweetie?"

"It's been fine. It's just... work. Go in, serve customers, collect tips, then go home. It's the same thing every day."

"Are you saving money?"

"Am I saving money?" Julie responded, as if she couldn't believe the question. She asked, "Why are you asking? Are we broke or something? You need a loan?"

Reina finally glanced back at her daughter. Although her daughter was wearing her plain uniform, she couldn't help but smile—she was an angel in her eyes.

She said, "We can always use a little extra cash, but I think I have everything under control right now. I just wanted to make sure you were still saving up for college. It's been a while since we've talked about it. Your plans haven't changed, have they?"

"Nope. I'm still saving money. I can't really afford to do anything fun, but... yeah, I'm saving."

"Good, good," Reina said as she turned her attention to her phone. As she punched some numbers into the calculator app, she asked, "How did you get home tonight? I didn't hear a car outside."

Julie bit her bottom lip and took a step back. Running to her room seemed like a decent idea—childish but decent.

She said, "I took the bus. Listen, um... I'm tired so I'm just going to–"

From the kitchen archway, Nick said, "I saw Daniel's car outside earlier."

Reina stopped tapping her phone. Stony-faced, she turned towards her daughter. She loved the girl, but she made some *very* bad decisions in her life.

Reina said, "You know what I think about Daniel, Julie. I've asked you to stop seeing him hundreds of times now."

Julie responded, "He's not that bad. You act like he beats me or something."

"He doesn't beat you, but his mistakes will destroy you. Believe me, I went through the same thing with your father. He–"

"I don't want to talk about dad."

"Fine, we won't talk about your dad. We have to talk about *your* decisions, though. Like I said, he might not be trying to hurt you, but it'll be hard to get past his mistakes. I mean, imagine if he gets you pregnant. He's not going to stop smoking, snorting, or... or... or 'popping pills' for you. He's going to end up in prison and you'll end up having to take care of a child on your own. He's stopping you from meeting your full potential, sweetie. You can do so much better."

Julie could argue with the best of them, but she decided to bite her tongue. She agreed with her mother's assessment anyway. *Daniel is an idiot,* she thought, *but he can still be saved.* She wasn't interested in having the same conversation with her mother, though.

From the archway, Nick grimaced and said, "Sorry." Julie looked over at her brother and pouted. Nick said, "It's just... He's an asshole, Julie."

"Nick, please watch your mouth," Reina said. She stared at her daughter with disappointment in her eyes. She whispered, "What am I going to do with you?"

Julie responded, "I know what I'm doing. I mean, I appreciate how you guys look after me, but... I *know* what I'm doing. Don't worry, I can handle my own life. I'm going to my room now. I need some rest. Good night."

Reina sighed, then she said, "Okay, I guess we'll talk about this later. Good night, sweetie. I love you. You know I love you, right?"

"I know! Love you, too!" Julie shouted as she walked down the hall.

There were five doors in the hallway. The first door to the right led to the bathroom. The second door to the right led to Julie's bedroom. The first door to the left opened up to a small storage closet. The second door to the left led to Nick's bedroom. The door at the end of the hall led to the master bedroom, which also had its own bathroom.

Julie marched into her bedroom. She closed the door and turned the lock, then she leaned back on the door and loudly exhaled—*relieved.*

As she ran her eyes over the poster-covered walls, she whispered, "Now I'm home..."

***

Across from the foot of the bed, music blared from

a set of speakers beside a computer on top of a desk. It was some modern R&B song. The music was loud enough to mask the other noises in the bedroom—the creaky floorboards, the squeaky mattress, *Julie's sexual moans.*

Julie lay in bed, sweat glistening across her body. She only wore a white tank top and her underwear. Her hand was shoved into her panties. She thrust her hips as she stroked her clitoris. Her breathing intensified as she reached her climax.

Her limbs stiffened and her body shuddered. Quavering breaths escaped her quivering lips. Euphoria flowed through her veins. She fought to keep her composure. Obviously, she didn't want her family to hear her orgasm. She blew out a sigh, relieved and pleased.

Julie could have had sex with Daniel. She loved him after all. She had a complicated relationship with men, though. She had sex before, but it never felt right. She was much more comfortable masturbating by her lonesome. Daniel couldn't pleasure her like her fingers anyway.

She glanced over at her door—it was still locked. She grabbed her phone from the nightstand and checked the time: *11:07 PM.* She looked around her dimly lit room. Everything looked normal. Yet, the room had an eerie vibe to it. It was a surreal feeling, as if she were conscious during a dream.

As she stared vacantly at the ceiling, Julie whispered, "Am I awake? Am I dreaming? Did I... Did I fall asleep? Shit, I really don't know..."

The R&B music slowed. It sounded distorted and choppy. The instruments *clashed* and *thumped.* The vocals were deep and melancholic.

Julie furrowed her brow and sat up in bed. The music player on the monitor looked normal. She assumed the problem was caused by the speakers. *The cable is loose,* she thought, *or the speakers are busted.* She looked for an explanation—*any explanation.*

She stood from her bed and approached the desk. The floorboards groaned under her bare feet with each step. As she reached the rolling chair, the music returned to normal.

Baffled, Julie whispered, "What the hell is going on here?" She gripped a handful of her hair as she thought about the situation. She murmured, "Is it... Is it a second-hand high? Is that even possible? Damn it, that stoner is really going to mess me up someday."

She leaned over her chair and turned off the computer. She couldn't help but tremble as the room became dead silent. As a matter of fact, the entire home felt inexplicably vacant. She knew her brother and mother were in their rooms, but it just didn't feel like it. She crossed her arms and rubbed her shoulders, overwhelmed by the eerie feeling.

As she turned and took her first step towards her bed, Julie stopped and stared at the window to her right. She froze in fear. A person appeared to be crouching outside of her window—the silhouette of a man. She couldn't see him, but her imagination ran wild.

She imagined a filthy roly-poly man crouching outside, vigorously masturbating with his hairy, sooty hands as drool dripped from his bottom lip. She pictured each bead of sweat racing down his greasy face while his thinning, wet hair fell over his forehead. For some odd reason, she imagined he would have red eyes, too—the eyes of a demon.

Her survival instincts told her to grab her phone and call 911 while screaming like a snobby child throwing a tantrum at the mall. Her naive curiosity told her to step forward and approach the window. She opted for the latter.

Legs like noodles, Julie reluctantly teetered towards the window. Hands over her chest, she breathed heavily as she slowly approached. She could feel the sweat streaming across her body, she could hear every *thumping* heartbeat in her chest. She crouched and pulled her shirt down over her thighs so the prowler wouldn't see her underwear.

She lunged forward and opened the blinds, then she weaved and bobbed her head for a better view. To her utter surprise, there was no one outside. The ominous silhouette vanished.

"It's all in my head," she said with a wry smile on her face.

Julie gasped as the sound of a creaky floorboard emerged from over her shoulder. She wasn't alone—and she knew that fact very well. *Please be Nick, please be Nick, please be Nick,* she thought. She breathed deeply as she slowly turned towards the noise. The farthest corner of the room was swallowed by an impenetrable darkness—darker than the bottom of the ocean.

She took a step forward, slow and calculated. The floorboards creaked under her foot. She took another cautious step, carefully approaching the corner. And, with each step, the outline of a dark humanoid figure became more defined in the darkness. The ominous figure was tall—at least a foot taller than her five-foot stature.

Julie stopped a meter away from the corner. As she gazed into the darkness, she stuttered, "Wha–What are you–"

Mid-sentence, she gasped and staggered in reverse as a man lunged at her from the shadows. She barely caught a glimpse of him. He wore tattered clothing—a threadbare button-up shirt and filthy jeans. His black hair was scruffy, wild and dirty. His face was distorted, though. She could only see his eyes. His eyes were completely black—no sclerae, no pupils, *just black.*

Julie tightly closed her eyes and grimaced as she was violently hurled into the air. Her stomach turned as she spun 180-degrees in mid-air. She didn't see herself spinning, but she could feel it. She grunted as she landed face-first on her bed. She was temporarily dazed by the unexpected attack. She couldn't understand what was happening.

She thought: *I didn't even see him touch me. How did he throw me in the air like that? What's happening to me?*

She squirmed on her stomach as she felt a powerful grip on the back of her head. Her face was pushed down into her pillow. She couldn't break free from the grip, either. The intruder was stronger than any man she had ever encountered. She cried into her pillow as she felt her underwear sliding down her legs.

She gasped—both from shock and a lack of oxygen—as her ass was spanked. Her underwear was pulled down to her ankles, stretched thin as her legs were forcibly separated. She whimpered into her pillow, horrified and confused. She knew what was going to happen, but she didn't know how to react.

Her Suffering   13

She didn't have the opportunity to fight back, either.

She gasped again as she felt pressure in her vagina. The intruder penetrated her. She had sex before, so she knew the feeling—it was certainly a penis. She panted and whimpered in pain with each rough thrust. Her muffled cries barely seeped past her pillow.

She could have tried to scream, but she didn't want to awaken her family. She didn't enjoy the assault—it broke her heart and destroyed her faith in humanity. She was just embarrassed. She didn't want her brother or mother to witness the attack. She didn't know how to deal with the harrowing situation. She figured she'd cooperate and wait until he was finished. She only wanted to survive at the moment.

Julie continued to cry into her pillow as she was ruthlessly attacked. She could feel the intruder's penis pounding her cervix, as if he were purposely trying to hurt her—trying to show off his size. She endured the pain, though, counting each passing second. Those seconds felt like hours to her. After a minute of thrusting, she felt a warm sensation in her vagina, then the penis vanished.

She didn't feel the penis as it actually withdrew, though. It felt like it just dissolved inside of her, turning into *nothing.* The grip on the back of her head was gone. The figure's presence immediately vanished, too. The bedroom no longer felt malevolent. She could even hear the floorboards and pipes in the other rooms. The home was normal.

Teary-eyed, Julie lifted her head from the pillow and glanced around the room—it was empty. She sniveled as she lifted her underwear up to her waist, then she curled into the fetal position. She constantly twitched and squirmed, struggling to calm her nerves. She didn't blame herself for the attack, but she still felt filthy. Her body was invaded, but the circumstances were bizarre.

As tears streamed down her cheeks, Julie stuttered, "D–Did... Did... Did it even happen? Oh, God, did it actually happen? Was that... Was it real?" She panted and sobbed, then she whispered, "What happened to me? What the hell just happened to me?"

Julie spent the night crying, lost in her thoughts. She thought about the intruder, the attack, and the drugs, trying her best to form a logical explanation. She didn't sleep a wink that night.

Chapter Two

Good Morning

At the stove, Reina cooked scrambled eggs and bacon while water boiled in the kettle. Nick sat at the kitchen table nearby, eating pancakes while flicking his finger across his cell phone's touchscreen. The irresistible scent of fresh breakfast meandered through the home. They figured the smell would be enough to wake Julie.

Reina glanced back at the table and asked, "How are the pancakes, Nicky?"

As he shoved a chunk of pancakes into his mouth, Nick said, "Good."

With a hand on her hip, Reina turned towards the table, puckered her lips, and tapped her foot. Her son appeared to be glued to his cell phone. Nick ate while he cycled through his social network apps. He could only do so much with his limited attention span.

Reina smiled and said, "Put it away, Nicky. Focus on eating. Come on, talk to me." She turned towards the stove and continued cooking. She said, "I don't want to hear anymore one-word responses from you unless I'm asking yes-or-no questions. So, how are you doing in school?"

Nick sighed as he turned off his phone's screen. He glanced over at his mother. The woman slaved away in the kitchen to make breakfast for her family, sacrificing her valuable time for her kids—and she never complained about it. He admired her for her dedication.

He said, "It's the same. You got my last report card, right?"

"Yeah—A's and B's. You still keeping that up?"

"Yep."

The one-word response brought a big smile to Reina's face. She was proud of her son's academic achievements. She hoped he would be eligible for financial aid in order to lessen the burden on their finances. Regardless, she was willing to work *every* day for the rest of her life to get her children through college.

Reina said, "That's great, hun. You know, I don't think I've asked you this since you were a little kid: what do you, *Nicky,* want to do when you grow up?"

Nick shrugged and said, "I don't know. I've never thought about it."

"You've never thought about it? Come on, every kid has dreams. You must have thought of something."

"Nope. I've never thought of it."

"Well, you still have plenty of time," Reina responded as she filled a mug with boiling water. She smirked and said, "Just make sure you pick something that will make you *a lot* of money. I'm not greedy or anything like that, but... money rules the world. Money can change everything, you know? It can't make you happy if you're just a miserable person or if you have the worst luck, but it can really make things easier. Yeah, pick something where the money is good so it's easier for you to be happy. I wish I did that..."

As he took a bite of his pancakes, Nick said, "I don't know. I want to make stuff, like movies and shows. I just, you know, want to make my own stuff. I think that would be cool. I don't know, though. I'm just saying..."

Reina glanced back at him, surprised. Acquiring his dream-job wouldn't be easy, but she would gladly help him with his journey. *He's a little artist,* she thought.

She smiled and said, "That's nice, Nick. Don't stop following your dreams, hun."

The pair glanced over at the archway near the front door as Julie walked past the kitchen. Julie, dressed in her diner uniform, hurriedly walked towards the door with her head down. She wasn't in the mood to talk.

Reina said, "*Wait.*"

Julie stopped in her tracks, just one meter away from the door. She stared at the golden doorknob and thought about running out despite her mother's order. *I'm an adult,* she thought, *I don't have to stick around if I don't want to.* She didn't have the common teenage attitude, though. She respected her mother too much to disobey her orders without reason.

She returned to the archway and asked, "What do you need?"

Reina said, "Well, good morning to you, too, Julie."

"Good morning, mom. Do you need help with anything? I really have to get to work."

"No, no. I just wanted to know if you wanted anything for breakfast. I made enough eggs and bacon for both of us. It would be nice if we could sit down and eat."

"Yeah, that would be nice, but I have to catch the bus."

"The bus? You don't have to take the bus, sweetie. Sit down and grab a bite to eat. I'll give you a ride in twenty, maybe thirty minutes. It'll still be a lot faster than the bus."

Julie rubbed her forehead with her fingertips, frustrated. She said, "I'd rather walk to the bus stop. It's nothing against you or your cooking or anything like that. I just need some fresh air and some time to think. Okay?"

Reina furrowed her brow and cocked her head back, baffled by her daughter's behavior. Although she became upset at times, Julie wasn't exactly an overly anxious or hostile teenager.

Reina asked, "Is something wrong?"

Julie thought about telling her mother the truth. At heart, she wanted to run into her mother's arms and tell her about the rape—a rape she couldn't explain. She couldn't muster the courage to tell her, though. She didn't want to talk about it in front of her younger brother, either. So, she frowned and remained quiet.

Breaking the silence, Nick stared down at his plate and said, "I heard her crying last night." He didn't tell on his sister because he was obnoxious, he was just looking out for her. He sighed, then he said, "I heard you when I was going to the bathroom."

Reina turned towards her son and asked, "*What?* What are you talking about? Why didn't you say anything last night?"

"I don't know. I guess I wasn't sure. I was going to go in to check on her, but the door was locked."

Reina asked, "What's going on, Julie? Is everything okay? Are you–" Wide-eyed, she stopped as a thought dawned on her. She wagged her finger at her daughter and asked, "Did you break up with Daniel?"

No, mom, I was attacked and you didn't notice—for a moment, Julie considered blurting out the insensitive response. She kept a straight face, though, fighting to keep her semblance of control afloat. She couldn't justifiably blame her mother for something she didn't understand. She took a deep breath to calm her nerves.

Lying through her teeth, she said, "We didn't break up. We just got into a little fight last night. I... I don't know what will happen between us, but... it's not looking good. I don't know." She glared at her mother as she tried to keep her act from crumbling. She asked, "Does that make you happy? Hmm? It's what you always wanted, right?"

In a soft tone, Reina responded, "No. No, not at all, sweetheart. I'd rather see you happy with him than miserable by yourself. You know that."

"Whatever. It doesn't matter. I have to go, okay? I'll see you tonight."

"Okay, alright. Call if you need anything."

"Yeah, sure..."

Julie waved at her family and rolled her eyes as she marched away from the archway. She didn't want to act like a child, but she believed it was her only option. She staggered onto the porch, mentally exhausted but relieved. She teetered across the walkway, struggling to keep her balance. *I'll tell her if it happens again,* she thought, *it was probably just a nightmare.*

In the kitchen, Reina smiled at her son and said, "Thank you for speaking up, sweetie. It's important to take care of each other. Families stick together, no matter what."

As he stabbed his pancakes with his fork, Nick asked, "Do you think she's mad at me?"

"Probably. Don't worry about it, though. She's probably going to feel better later knowing she got that off her chest."

"I wasn't trying to get her in trouble or anything."

"She's not in trouble," Reina said as she turned towards her son. She could see the guilt sitting on his shoulders. She smiled and said, "You did good, Nicky. You really are the man of the house. Come on, you should start getting ready for school. I'll eat, then I'll drive you."

"Okay..."

Chapter Three

The Diner

Julie shambled from table-to-table, delivering meals and drinks to her customers. She smiled when she approached each table, trying to appear happy and welcoming. She depended on her customers' tips after all, so she had to please them with her service. Fear still poisoned her heart and doubt still clouded her mind, though. She felt as if she had spent the entire morning acting in a movie, playing the role of a woman who *wasn't* attacked.

Julie approached the kitchen pass-through window and clipped the most recent order onto the rotating metal ring, which was used by the cooks in the kitchen to keep track of the orders. She hit the call-bell twice—*we have another one.* Since the lunch rush was slowing to a crawl, she leaned on the counter and doodled on her notepad. She tried drawing the person from the previous night, but she had trouble remembering his face.

She thought: *who are you? Were you even real?*

"Hey!" a female voice enthusiastically said from over her shoulder.

Julie glanced back and smiled. Tracy, a close friend and co-worker, stood at the kitchen doorway. Her dark, wavy hair bounced on her shoulders as she shook her head and giggled. She was puckish, always finding light in the dark, so she recognized Julie's distant attitude. Seeing a grown woman mope like a child made her laugh. Of course, she didn't actually know the severity of Julie's situation.

Tracy approached the counter and said, "You've been quiet since you got here, Julie. What's wrong? Did you get rejected by some pretentious college or something?"

Julie responded, "No. I'm just... I don't know, Tracy. I... I was... I'm not really in the mood to talk about it."

"Okay. Well, if you're ever in the mood to talk about 'it,' you know I'm here for you. You should try cheering up, though. The boss-man might make you clean shit off the toilets if you're not at least *pretending* to be happy."

Julie said, "I know, I know. I'm trying. It's just–" She stopped as she heard the door chime—another customer had arrived. She glanced at Tracy and said, "I've got this one."

Tracy cracked a smile and took a step back, allowing Julie to walk past her. She stared at her seemingly depressed friend with a furrowed brow. She opened her mouth to speak, but she couldn't say a word before Julie walked past her.

Notepad in hand, Julie approached the front door. She slowed her march to a stroll as she neared the entrance of the diner.

A man stood near the front door. The man had curly black hair, dark brown eyes, and stubble on his chiseled jawline. He wore a button-up shirt with the sleeves rolled up, blue jeans, and boots. He retained his youth—he appeared to be in his late thirties, but he had a youthful aura to him. He was handsome and charismatic, too.

Julie wasn't drawn to him because of his charm, though. She thought she recognized him, but she couldn't put a name to his face.

Julie said, "Welcome to Alfonso's Diner. Would you like to sit at the bar, a table, or a booth?"

With a soft, honeyed voice, the man asked, "I can sit anywhere?"

"Yeah. Usually, if you're alone, we would sit you at the bar, but it's not busy now so you can pick. What will it be, sir?"

"A booth. I'd like to sit at a booth. They remind me of the good ol' days."

"Okay, sure. Follow me."

Julie grabbed a menu from a rack near the foyer of the diner, then she walked towards the end of the dining area. She beckoned to the enigmatic patron, leading him to the last booth.

As the man took his seat, Julie placed the menu on the table and said, "I'll give you some time to look over the menu, unless you're already ready to order. I can get a drink for you now if you want."

"Coffee. I'll have coffee."

"Okay, I'll bring that right out for you. Let me know if you need anything else."

"Will do, babe, will do."

Babe—Julie raised her brow upon hearing the word. It wasn't exactly a catcall, but the word still caused her to shudder. She couldn't tell if the eerie sensation was caused by the word or his voice—*or both.* She faked a smile and nodded at the man, then she walked away.

As Julie filled a mug with coffee at the counter, Tracy asked, "What are you doing?"

Julie smiled and responded, "Working hard. I think I'm dealing with another old guy who still thinks he's a player. What's up with these creeps, huh?"

"Wha–What?"

"I'll tell you about it after I get him his coffee, *babe*."

Julie giggled as she walked away from the counter. She returned to the booth and placed the coffee on the table while the man examined the menu.

Julie said, "Here's your coffee, sir. The creamer and the sugar are to your left if you need it. Call me when you're ready to order."

"Thank you very much," the man said as he reached for his coffee. As Julie took her first step away from the booth, the patron asked, "Have we met? Hmm? I mean, have I ever seen you before?"

Julie stopped and looked back at him. She smiled and said, "It's funny you say that. I have no idea, but I could have sworn I've seen you somewhere before, too."

"Yeah. It's hard to tell, isn't it? It would be strange if you were the person I was thinking about, wouldn't it?"

"Why do you say that?"

"Well, because I *just* saw the person I'm thinking about last night. I was... you know, making sweet love to her. She was a young woman, like yourself. I'm not one to kiss-and-tell, but... I really gave it to her. I pushed her face down into the pillow and I fucked that tight pussy. I really *pounded* it. It was good for me, I'm not sure if I can say the same for her."

The man chuckled and shook his head, as if he remembered something embarrassing. He took a loud sip of his coffee, the *slurp* echoing through the diner. Julie took another step away from the booth, unnerved by the man's inappropriate speech. The patron spoke as if he knew about what happened to Julie—and Julie couldn't comprehend it.

She thought: *was he the one who attacked me? Was he in my room last night? Did he follow me here?*

She opened her mouth to speak, but she could only croak and groan. Her bottom lip quivered and tears welled over in her eyes. She stared at the man in disbelief. To her dismay, she could no longer recognize him. The man's face became warped. His eyes, nose, mouth, and facial hair blended with his skin until his face was a blank canvas of beige flesh.

Julie tightly closed her eyes and stuttered, "C-Call... Call me if–if you need anything."

As Julie walked away, the man responded, "Oh, I'll call you when I'm ready, baby. And, don't worry about a thing: I'll be ready soon, Julie."

Julie stopped in place before she could reach the counter. Panicked breaths escaped her pink lips. Goosebumps formed on her arms and the hairs on the back of her neck prickled. She had a few options on the table: confront the man in a heated confrontation, run out the front door and head home, or walk behind the counter and call the cops.

With Tracy and her coworkers nearby, calling the cops seemed like the best option. She walked around the counter and hurried to the cash register. With a trembling hand, she grabbed the phone and held it up to her ear.

As Julie dialed 911, Tracy approached and said, "Wait, Julie. What are you doing? Who are you serving?"

"A pig. A fucking pig."

"*A pig?*" Tracy repeated, doubt in her voice. She closed her eyes and shook her head. She pulled the phone away from her friend and asked, "Are you playing some sort of game or something? What's wrong with you?"

Julie glared at Tracy and responded, "What's wrong with *me?* I'm serving some perverted pig, Tracy. I think he was the one in–"

She stopped mid-sentence. She leaned to her left and stared at the last booth in the diner. To her utter surprise, the booth was empty. A mug filled with coffee and a menu sat on the table, but there was no one in sight. The man was never there. Some of the other patrons stared at her, too, baffled by her erratic behavior. *They all saw me talking to myself,* she thought, *but they didn't see him.*

Pale-faced as if she had seen a ghost, Julie turned towards Tracy and said, "I have to talk to you about something *very* important. When the guys come in for their shifts, get your break with me. Okay?"

Tracy slowly nodded and said, "Okay, sure. I'll see what I can do."

***

Julie and Tracy met outside of the diner for their fifteen-minute break. Julie leaned on the wall near the back door with her arms crossed, visibly absent. Tracy stood in front of her friend, smoking a cigarette as she analyzed Julie's peculiar behavior. They didn't say anything.

The sound of coughing engines and people chattering emerged from the neighboring streets— the diner sat near the corner of a busy intersection. The noise didn't bother them, though. In fact, the ruckus was welcomed with open arms. The noise would mask their conversation after all.

Tracy took a puff of her cigarette, then she asked, "So, why'd you put that mug on the table?"

I'm going insane—Julie thought it was the most

fitting response. It was difficult to admit, though. One thought led to another and she was soon self-diagnosing herself with a mental disorder. It wasn't right.

As she wagged her cigarette, Tracy said, "It was weird. You went to the front door of the diner, grabbed a menu, walked to the booth, talked to yourself, then you took a mug to the table... What was up with that? Are you, um, not getting enough sleep? Or did Daniel lace his weed with PCP again? You know that will fuck your mind up, right?"

Julie nervously laughed and nodded. Tracy didn't say anything funny, but it was the first response that came to mind.

She asked, "Can... Can I tell you a secret? It's going to sound crazy, like completely insane, but you have to promise not to tell anyone. I don't give a crap if you laugh, but you *can't* tell anyone. Okay?"

"You know you can trust me, Jules. When have I ever gossiped about you? Come on, talk to me. What's wrong?"

Julie trusted Tracy. She had no reason to *distrust* her. The pair had been friends since middle school. They were even saving up their money in hopes of moving in together when Julie went to college.

Julie said, "I was with Daniel last night. He smoked, I didn't. I don't think he smoked anything but weed. He just packed a bowl and smoked. It was clean and safe. Even if I somehow got a 'contact high,' that was *last* night. So, if you think I was hallucinating because of laced weed, you're wrong. It just wouldn't make sense. I couldn't still be feeling the side-effects, right?"

"I guess you're right. So, what happened in there?

What did you see exactly?"

"What did I see? Well, um..."

Rosy-cheeked, Julie frowned and looked down at her shoes. She felt as if she were taking her first step towards admitting she was crazy. It was a difficult step to take, especially during a time of uncertainty.

She said, "I saw a man in the diner, Tracy. When I saw him, I swear I instantly recognized him—and he recognized me. There was a... a connection. I saw him very clearly, but I couldn't put a name to his face. It was so weird." She sighed and shook her head, disappointed. She said, "Listen, I know he wasn't actually there. I understand that now. But you have to understand something, too: it all felt *so* real. You didn't see him, but I did. He was there and he was... He... He was there, okay?"

Julie wanted to say: *he was there and he was evil.* She was already giving her best friend a lot to digest, so she figured she'd wait until she saw her reaction to her bizarre story before adding more strange details to her tale.

Tracy stared at her friend with a deadpan expression. She didn't laugh at her, though. She didn't even crack a smile. She took another puff of her cigarette, the cherry glowing like a torch at night.

Tracy said, "Okay, I think I get it. So, why do you think you saw him?"

Julie responded, "I'm not 100-percent sure, but... it might have something to do with something else. You see, something happened to me last night and it was just as strange as this. No, it was worse. It was so much worse."

"What happened?"

A frog in her throat, Julie explained, "Well, I was... I

was in my room last night. It was, like, 11:00 PM or something. Some weird shit happened, then I thought I saw someone in the... the corner of my room. I don't know how he got there, but just like in the diner, *he was there.*"

Cigarette burning in her hand, Tracy stared at Julie with a raised brow. She was blatantly astonished by the story, unable to utter a word.

Her voice cracking, Julie continued, "This man—or this *thing*—attacked me. He threw me onto my bed, he..." She paused and sniffled, fighting the urge to cry. She leaned closer to Tracy and whispered, "He took off my underwear, then he... he 'assaulted' me. He *invaded* me, Tracy. When he finished, I turned around and he was gone. I don't know how to explain it, but it happened. And, I feel like that person I saw in the diner was the same thing that attacked me last night. I can feel it in my heart."

The cigarette fell to the floor and Tracy giggled. She hunched forward and stepped back as she cackled. The story was frightening, but she didn't believe it. To most people, ghosts were fictional entities used in movies and books to scare people. Ghosts didn't haunt suburban houses, ghosts didn't *rape* innocent teenagers.

As she recomposed herself, Tracy said, "Wait, wait, wait... Are you saying you were, like, sexually assaulted by a ghost? Oh, God, that's gold. How the hell did you come up with that?"

Julie remained stern and quiet. The laughing didn't hurt her. As a matter of fact, it was the exact reaction she expected. Upon noticing her friend's silence, Tracy stopped laughing. She gazed into Julie's eyes and grimaced. She could see she wasn't lying.

Tracy said, "You're serious..." She shoved her fingers into her hair as her lips sank and formed a frown. She said, "Okay, um... *Okay.* I don't know much about ghosts and all that crap, but I've taken a Psychology class and I've, you know, seen some documentaries. If you didn't see anyone in the house, if it was *impossible* for him to be there, then I think it was a hallucination. It was probably because of the weed. I know you didn't smoke, but maybe just the idea of smoking and getting caught made you more anxious than usual."

"No, I don't think so. I tried to convince myself it was the drugs, I really wanted to believe it was a–a 'contact high,' but that's not it. I'd just be lying to myself."

"Okay, maybe it was a dream. Haven't you ever had one of those dreams where you had wild sex? You know, some crazy, passionate sex?"

"This wasn't passionate. It was... It was *rape.* And, even if it was a dream, it doesn't explain why I brought a damn mug to an empty booth and talked to myself for a minute."

Tracy said, "You should tell your mom."

"*No,*" Julie snapped, glaring at her friend with a set of furious eyes. She shook her head and said, "I can't tell my mom and you can't tell her, either. Okay? Promise me you won't tell her, Tracy. *Promise me.*"

"Okay, okay. I promise. You have to tell someone, though. I'm not really helping you, I'm not a professional. Maybe you should go see a doctor. Or, if you really think it's something... 'supernatural,' maybe you should see a priest. It's not like they have to tell your mom, right? You're technically an adult already, so you don't need your mom's consent or anything."

Julie crossed her arms and rubbed her shoulders as she considered her options. A visit to a doctor was out of the question—one way or another, her mother would find out. She wasn't religious so she didn't know any priests. She thought: *what would I even say?* 'Hello, Father, I was raped by a ghost. Can you help me?' It didn't seem like a helpful option.

Julie said, "I don't know what I'm going to do. I'm just... I'm going to stay away from Daniel and his drugs for a while. If I keep seeing things, I guess I'll go see a doctor."

"Good. I'll go with you, too. Just let me know ahead of time. You don't have to do this alone," Tracy responded. She crushed her cigarette with her foot, then she said, "We should go back inside. Come on, break time is over."

Julie smiled and nodded, reassured by her friend's kind offer. The pair returned to the diner, prepared to finish their shifts.

Chapter Four

Welcome Home

Julie quietly closed the front door. On her tiptoes, she slinked towards the kitchen archway and peeked into the room—it was empty. She could hear the television in the living room, though. *Nick is in his room,* she thought, *mom is in the living room.* She crept towards the hall to the right, lunging over the squeaky floorboards. As expected, her mother sat in the living room and riffled through a stack of papers.

As Julie took her first step into the hall, Reina said, "Julie, don't go to your room yet." She glanced over at her daughter and smiled. She said, "You can't get away from me, sweetie. I know you too well. Or, maybe it's just my mother's intuition. I always know when you're around."

Julie walked back to the living room. With half a smile, she said, "Hey, mom. How's it going?"

"It's going... well. I have some paperwork to deal with for Tim, but I think it can wait until tomorrow. I *hope* it can wait until tomorrow 'cause I'm exhausted."

Reina dug her fingers into her hair and turned in her seat, one leg folded under her. She smiled as she stared at her daughter—a working woman just like her. Julie returned the smile, proud of her mother. Her mother worked for a real estate firm, so she was always busy, but she never forgot about her family. Her mother's intuition was always on the clock.

Reina asked, "How was your day?"

"It was fine. It was just another day, like yesterday and tomorrow."

"Yeah, I know what you mean. Did you eat? Want me to cook something up?"

"No, no. It's okay. I grabbed a bite to eat at the diner."

"Are you sure? I can heat up some leftovers if you want. It won't take more than five minutes."

Julie couldn't help but giggle. Mothers always seemed to be so persistent when it came to food—Reina was no different.

Julie said, "I'm fine, really. I'm just a little tired. I think I'm just going to go rest in my room. I could use a nap."

"Okay. Go get some rest, baby. Let me know if you need anything. I love you."

As she walked down the hall, Julie responded, "I love you, too, mom."

Julie pushed her door open. She stood in the doorway and gazed into her dimly lit room. The room looked normal—everything in its rightful place. Yet, a malevolent aura still lingered in the bedroom. She *felt* the evil lurking in her room, hiding in the shadows and waiting for the perfect opportunity to strike.

It's still here, she thought, *it's been waiting for me, hasn't it?*

"What are you looking at?" Nick asked, standing in the hall near his bedroom.

Julie hopped and gasped, startled by her brother's sudden appearance in the hall. She held her hand over her chest and breathed deeply as she recomposed herself.

She stuttered, "N–Nothing. I... I just got a little

lightheaded."

"Are you okay?"

"I'm fine, squirt. I'm going to take a nap and I'll be back to normal," Julie responded. She ruffled his hair and pushed him towards the living room. She said, "Go get your snack or whatever you were going to do."

"I was going to get some water."

"Go. I'll see you later, kiddo."

Baffled by the awkward exchange, Nick said, "Okay, later..."

Keeping a fake smile on her face, Julie slipped into her bedroom. She didn't close the door, though. She left the door cracked open, allowing the light from her room to pour into the hallway. It was only an inch, but it made her feel safe. She gladly sacrificed her privacy for a sense of security.

She dropped her bag on the foot of the bed, then she sat down on the rolling chair in front of her computer. Her fingers hovered over the keyboard as she stared at the monitor. The web browser was opened to Google. The cursor blinked in the text box, waiting to leave a trail of words behind it.

She knew what she wanted to search, but, at the back of her mind, she feared someone was monitoring her online activities. She figured they used an automated system, but she still believed the government was watching everyone—and that was frightening.

She thought: *how embarrassing would it be if they read all of my searches?*

She took a deep breath and shrugged off the thoughts. She searched: *ghost attacks.* The results, consisting of compilations of ghost attacks 'caught on camera,' were disappointing. She deleted the search and stared at the blinking cursor. She typed: *Ghost.* She stopped herself before she could type the second word: *rape.*

Ghost rape.

She knew the entity actually raped her, but she was too afraid to admit it—even to a search engine. The idea was absurd and horrifying. She believed it was absurd because it related to ghosts. Ghosts were like zombies to her—characters created for horror fiction. Yet, she was still terrified because she *knew* it happened to her. She was attacked by something she couldn't identify.

As she stared at the monitor, Julie placed her chin on her palms and whispered, "What am I doing? I'm actually searching for ghosts. Maybe I should be searching for... for mental illness. I'm crazy, aren't I? What am I going to do? What–"

She stopped as a shrill *squealing* sound emerged in the room. *The hinges,* she thought. She slowly turned her head, as if she didn't want to look back. She couldn't stop herself, though. Curiosity got the best of her. Stiff like a corpse, she glanced over her shoulder and stared at the door.

The door slowly swung open, as if someone had pushed it with a gentle hand. There was no one there, though. The door stopped, then a floorboard *creaked.* It sounded as if someone had stepped into the room. A cool breeze blew into the bedroom from the doorway, too.

Eyes welling over with tears, Julie stuttered, "I–Is... Is someone... Is someone there?"

She gasped and rolled back in her seat as the door slammed shut. The doorknob jiggled and the walls trembled due to the sheer force. The lock on the door turned by itself, sealing the young woman in her bedroom. The sound of floorboards groaning followed, growing louder with each passing second. It sounded like someone was approaching the desk.

Before she could scream or run, Julie felt an inexplicable pressure on her abdomen, as if someone were touching her. She stared down at her shirt, tears dripping from her eyes. She could see the imprint of a large hand on her button-up shirt. *An invisible man,* she thought, *oh, God, it's going to happen again.*

She felt the same pressure on the small of her back. Her stomach turned as she was lifted from the chair. She appeared to be levitating, but she could feel the hands on her body.

Julie shouted, "Mom! Help! Mom, please!"

She shrieked as she soared across the room, hurled with ease like a baseball. She grunted as she landed on her back on her bed. She squirmed in reverse until the back of her head hit the headrest. Her eyes widened as the mattress sank around her. It looked like someone had climbed onto the bed with her.

Julie stammered, "N–No, no, no. Please, not again. Don't–"

She coughed and sniffled as she felt a strong grip around her neck, like if someone was strangling her. She couldn't scream. She could only croak and groan. She couldn't move, either. She felt as if she were being held down by a horde of powerful men. Her limbs were pinned to the mattress and the grip around her neck remained strong.

Eyes wide with fear, she stared down at her body. Her skirt was pushed up to her waist, revealing her white panties. Her underwear was torn from her body, ripped with one powerful tug. Her legs were pushed away from each other. She gritted her teeth as the entity penetrated her. She couldn't see him, but he felt large—and it hurt.

She turned her head and looked over at the door as the mysterious entity continued to violently thrust into her. Her brain throbbed, her ears rang, and her vision blurred, but she wasn't dead. Although barely visible and faint, she could *see* the doorknob rattling and she could *hear* her mother screaming in the hallway.

In a croaky tone, Julie whispered, "Mom... Mom, help me. I can't... I can't breathe." She sobbed, warm tears rolling down to her ears and plopping on her pillow. She whispered, "Help me. I don't want to die..."

In the hallway, Reina rammed the door with her shoulder and frantically shook the knob—but to no avail. She put all of her energy and weight behind each tackle, but it wouldn't budge.

Standing in the corridor, baffled and terrified, Nick asked, "What's happening to her?"

Reina shouted, "Go get the keys from my room! They're on the dresser! Hurry!"

Nick glanced at the door, then at his mother, then back at the door. He couldn't connect the pieces, he didn't understand the situation.

Reina yelled, "Now, Nick! *Hurry!*"

As Nick sprinted down the hall, Reina knocked on the door and shouted, "Julie! Julie, what's wrong? Answer me, baby. Julie, say something!"

It started with a scream: *Mom! Help! Mom, please!* Reina immediately bolted to her daughter's bedroom from the living room. The door was locked, though. So, she tackled the door and shook the knob, but the effort was fruitless. By then, her daughter was no longer screaming. She didn't hear her speak or even whisper.

She could only hear Julie's painful whimpers and a constant *thumping* sound. It felt like an eternity listening to her child cry in the bedroom. It felt the same for Julie, except she was being defiled.

Reina felt helpless and hopeless in the hallway. A door—a *measly* door—stopped her from protecting her daughter. *What kind of mother am I?*—she thought.

As he approached his mother, Nick shouted, "Here!"

Reina turned towards her son, relieved. She took the keys and quickly unlocked the door, her fingers trembling uncontrollably in the process. She pushed the door open, prepared to rush into the room to help her daughter, but she stopped in the doorway—confused, surprised, *aghast.* Her jaw dangled open while her eyes widened.

Nick stood beside his mother, anxious to discover the truth. He looked over her shoulder and gazed into the room. His eyes practically bulged from his skull. He was a young teenager who grew up with the internet. He had seen unbelievable things before, but *nothing* could prepare him for the truth.

Julie lay on the bed, her arms and legs outstretched away from her body. She was nude from the waist down. The bed rocked under her, swaying left and right, and she shook with each imperceptible thrust. She had a hollow look in her eyes, as if she were already dead.

As the bed stopped shaking, Nick looked over at Julie's feet. He furrowed his brow and tilted his head.

The mattress *rose* as if someone had stood up from the bed. He didn't see anyone else in the room, though. He couldn't explain the phenomenon.

Julie gasped for air as the fierce grip around her neck finally loosened. Between breaths, she said, "Mom... Mom, help... Help me! Please!" She sat up on the bed with her knees to her face, twitching and shuddering. She shouted, "He's still here! He... He raped me! Oh, God, he... he... he raped me..."

Reina erratically blinked as she snapped out of her fear-induced trance. She turned towards her son, blocking his view of Julie.

She gently pushed him down the hall and said, "Go to your room and lock the door. *Now.*"

Nick took one final glance at Julie's room. He couldn't muster the courage to tell his mother about the mattress. He figured she had enough to handle without his bizarre claims. He reluctantly retreated to his bedroom.

Reina ran to her daughter's side. She sat down beside her, pulling Julie closer to her bosom. Julie cried hysterically into her mother's chest. She mumbled indistinctly as Reina stroked her hair and caressed her cheek.

Reina asked, "What's wrong, baby? What happened? Christ, what did you take?"

"*No,* this... this wasn't be–because of drugs," Julie sternly said as she pulled away from Reina's chest.

She glared at her mother, infuriated by the offensive assumption. She couldn't blame her, though. She couldn't see her attacker, so she didn't think her family could see him, either. It sounded crazy—and she understood that. She grimaced and cried, unable to endure the physical and emotional pain. She was devastated by the brutal attack.

In a raspy voice, she said, "I... I was raped, mom. Someone attacked me in here. It wasn't drugs. I swear it wasn't drugs. He... He really raped me." She glanced around the room until she spotted her ripped underwear on the floor. She said, "*Look.* I... I didn't rip my own underwear off, mom. I was attacked. You have to believe me."

Reina stared down at the underwear. She thought: *anyone could rip a pair of panties, right?* She glanced around the room, but she didn't see anyone. The window was closed and the door was locked before she entered the room. There was no way a man was in the room with her. *I would have seen him,* she thought, *Nick would have seen him.*

Still, she believed her daughter. She pulled the covers over Julie's lap, trying her best to cover her up, then she pulled her closer to her chest.

She kissed the top of her head, then she said, "Okay, okay. We're going to get to the bottom of this, okay? Don't cry, baby. You're safe now. I won't let anyone hurt you. I'm here, baby, I'm still here."

Reina hummed a melody—a lullaby her daughter loved as a child. She stared at the darkest corner of the room, curious but frightened. There was no one there, but she still felt a malevolent presence. She felt as if someone were staring back at her from the shadows.

As she gazed into the darkness, Reina said, "Everything's going to be okay, sweetie. I... I just have to call the police. They'll make sure we're safe. I know it."

Chapter Five

Did It Really Happen?

Red and blue lights flashed across the night sky, illuminating the street with vibrant colors. Two police cruisers were parked in front of the Knight home. A few neighbors, wrapped in their favorite robes, stood on their front lawns and watched the commotion from afar. People were naturally attracted to drama, especially when tragedy was involved.

Officer Connor Stone stood on the front lawn of the Knight home. Flashlight in hand, the young man examined the area outside of Julie's room. He illuminated her window and the flowerbed in front of the house. He diligently searched for fingerprints and footprints. He didn't find any evidence of an intruder outside, though. There wasn't a single smudge on the window, either.

"Nothing," Stone whispered, disappointed.

He leaned forward and peered through the window. He could barely see into the bedroom through the curtains and blinds. He spotted Julie on the bed, a towel draped over her shoulders and a blanket covering her body. He also spotted his partner, Dave Hames, standing near the doorway.

Hames spoke to Julie while examining the room. He didn't search every nook and cranny at the moment because the officers already checked the bedroom when they arrived. The officer's presence in the room was primarily used to make Julie feel safe and comfortable.

As he gazed at the tormented teenager, Stone murmured, "What happened to you, miss? Who hurt you?"

Stone walked into the house. He stopped at the first archway and looked into the kitchen. Nick sat at the kitchen table, alone and anxious. The boy was clearly traumatized by the strange event.

Stone asked, "How are you holding up, son?" Nick responded with a shrug. Stone said, "Don't worry. Everything is going to be okay. You're fine, you're safe. You have my word on that. I'm going to talk to your mother, alright? Keep your head up, son."

He nodded at the boy, then he walked to the hallway. Holding a piece of tissue paper over her nose, Reina leaned on the wall across from her daughter's room and stared at her doorway.

Stone said, "Ms. Knight, I think we should talk."

Reina kept her eyes locked on Julie's bedroom. Her stare was vacant, but her mind was flooded with terrifying thoughts.

Without taking her eyes off of the doorway, she asked, "What is it? Did you find anything? Are we safe here?"

"You're safe. I found nothing of significance outside."

"Then, what are you doing here? Shouldn't you be searching for... for... *for someone?*"

"That's what we need to talk about, ma'am. When we arrived, you told us the window was locked from the inside and you never saw anyone open it. You also said you—and your son—didn't see anyone in the room. Outside, there is *no* evidence of a peeping Tom, stalker, intruder, or whatever you'd like to call 'em. As of now, there is absolutely no evidence of a home invasion and there are no signs of forced entry. The ripped underwear qualifies as evidence, obviously, but that doesn't give us much to work with."

Reina wasn't surprised by the officer's conclusion. She called them based off a gut feeling. Despite the lack of evidence, her mother's intuition told her that her daughter was attacked and she had to do something about it. So, she called the police.

Stone continued, "We take calls of sexual assault very seriously, but there's not much we can do with what we have here. It would help if Julie would take a ride to the hospital, we could check out the bruises on her neck as well as her genitalia, but she has refused to get a medical examination. We can't force her, either. To be blunt with you, ma'am, I'm not even sure a medical examination of that sort would do anything since I'm not sure there's anything else to investigate."

Reina cocked her head back, astonished by the officer's audacity. She responded, "What? Are you saying my daughter lied? You think we made all of this up?"

Stone said, "No, ma'am. I don't believe she is intentionally lying. I've met victims of sexual assault before—and Julie reminds me of those legitimate victims. I'm not an expert in the field, but... maybe it was all in her head. Maybe it was a bad nightmare or a hallucination. You said it yourself, ma'am: you didn't see anyone in or around her room."

"I... I guess you're right, but... No, I trust my daughter. I didn't see anyone, but that doesn't mean he doesn't exist, right? That doesn't mean it didn't happen, right? He could have left before I got to the room. Maybe I was wrong, maybe the windows weren't locked."

Stone nodded, then he said, "I can continue investigating if you'd like. I can go outside and ask your neighbors if they saw a prowler near your home or any suspicious people in the neighborhood. I'm going to need your permission, though. If it *didn't* happen and if Julie *is* sick, I don't want to hurt her by helping to create rumors. I don't want to harm her in any way. So, would you like me to ask around?"

Reina considered the options. The officer clearly believed Julie was mentally ill. The evidence—or lack thereof—supported his theory. She couldn't accept it, though. Still, she didn't want to harm her daughter by facilitating gossip.

She said, "I think, um... I think I understand what you're saying. Would it be okay if you patrolled this area a little more tonight? Just in case? I mean, it would probably make her feel a lot better. She shouldn't be stressing out during a time like this."

"We can do that. I'll personally drive by your home every hour until the end of my shift," Stone said, reassuring the distressed mother. He glanced over at the doorway and thought about Julie's condition. He said, "In the meantime, I suggest you contact a professional in mental health. A psychologist, a psychiatrist... someone who can help her. And, if she really believes this happened, I hope you can convince her to get that medical examination so we can begin tracking the suspect. Okay?"

"I understand."

The officer sighed, then he said, "You have my card. Call if you need anything or if you'd like to talk. Every detail helps in cases like this, so, if you suddenly remember anything, don't hesitate." Stone beckoned to his partner and said, "Hames, let's go."

Reina waved and nodded as the officers walked past her in the hallway. She tried to crack a smile—an expression of gratitude and relief—but her daughter's questionable condition siphoned all of the happiness from her body. She walked behind the officers until they left her house, then she closed and locked the front door.

She placed her forehead on the door and whimpered. *How do you tell your daughter you couldn't help her?*–she thought. She couldn't think of a satisfying answer, she didn't know how to comfort Julie.

From the kitchen archway, Nick asked, "Is everything okay?"

Reina stopped whimpering upon hearing her son's tender voice. She refused to show weakness around him. As a single parent, she believed she was supposed to be perpetually strong. She sniffled and wiped the tears from her eyes, then she glanced back at her son with a slight smile on her face.

She said, "Everything's fine. Do me a favor, baby: go to your room and sleep. Okay?"

Through her fake smile, Nick could see the pain in his mother's eyes. Although he didn't believe her, he refused to challenge her.

He said, "Okay. Good night. I love you."

As Nick walked back to his room, Reina said, "I love you, too, sweetheart."

Reina shambled down the hallway. She stopped at Julie's bedroom. From the doorway, she stared at her troubled daughter with a set of glum eyes. Julie could see the disappointment and fear in her mother's eyes.

She frowned and looked away, realizing the police didn't believe her outlandish story.

Reina sat beside her daughter on the bed. Through the blanket and towel, which were tightly wrapped around her body, she stroked Julie's hair and forehead.

Julie asked, "They left, didn't they?"

"Yeah. The officer told me he would be driving by our house every hour until the end of his shift."

"But he didn't believe me, did he?"

"It's not that we don't believe you, Julie. It's just that... that they couldn't find any evidence of an intruder."

Julie pulled away from her mother. Depressed and exhausted, she gazed into Reina's eyes. She didn't know who to blame. *Is it my fault it attacked me? Is it my fault they don't believe me?*–she thought.

Julie asked, "Do you think I lied to you? Do you think I'm on drugs or something? 'Cause I'm not. Okay? *I'm not.*"

"I don't think you're on drugs, baby. You just have to look at it from our perspective. I didn't see anyone, Nick didn't see anyone, and even *you* didn't see anyone. No one saw a thing. That doesn't mean you didn't feel anything, but... we can't go around looking for an invisible man. You have to understand that, sweetie."

Puffy-eyed, Julie nodded and said, "I know it sounds crazy, but I really felt it, mom. It felt so real. Someone raped me. He came into my room, he ripped my underwear off, and he... he raped me. I could *feel* him inside of me. It hurt so much. I can... Shit, I can still feel it inside of me!"

Reina grimaced and sobbed, devastated by the

horrific statement. She wrapped her arms around her daughter's head and pulled her closer to her chest. The couple cried, creating a poignant symphony of melancholy. Sitting on the floor in front of his door, Nick held his hands over his face and cried. He could hear his family's weeping and it broke his heart.

Her voice cracking, Reina said, "Let me take you to a psychologist, sweetie. Please, let's go get some professional help."

Julie cried, "But it was real, mom. It... It was real, wasn't it?"

"If you believe it was real, then it was real. That doesn't mean we can't check for any other possibilities. Please, Julie, help me help you. *Please.*"

Julie stared at the darkest corner of her bedroom and considered her mother's suggestion. She feared the social stigmas associated with mental health. If someone saw her at a psychologist's office, she knew rumors would spread like a California wildfire. However, she feared the invisible intruder more than anything at the moment.

Julie said, "I'll go."

Reina kissed her daughter's forehead, then she said, "Thank you. Thank you so much."

Before her mother could stand up, Julie grabbed her gown and asked, "Mom, can I... can I sleep in your room tonight?"

"Of course, sweetie. We can share my bed. Come on, let's go to my room to get some rest. I'll call the doctor's office in the morning."

Reina held her daughter's hand and helped her stand from the bed. Julie staggered out of the room, a foot ahead of her mother. Reina stopped in the doorway and took one final glance into the bedroom.

She still felt the lingering malevolence. She closed the door, then the pair walked to the master bedroom—rattled by the horrific night.

Chapter Six

Hypnotherapy

Dr. Alexander Morris and Reina Knight stood in the gloomy hallway of a medical facility. Beside them, a door led to the doctor's office where Julie waited for an evaluation.

Morris was a middle-aged man, charming and compassionate. His soft blue eyes were gentle—not a glimmer of malevolence in sight. His grizzled hair was parted to the right, slick and professional. He wore a tweed jacket over a button-up shirt, brown pants, and matching dress shoes. He was the perfect doctor for Julie.

He said, "Ms. Knight, I intend on performing something called 'hypnotherapy' on your daughter. She has already agreed to it, but, first, I need to know a little more about Julie's medical background. I'd ask her, but, sometimes, patients tell white lies—innocent fibs. I'm not saying your daughter will lie to me, but she might not be completely honest out of embarrassment or shame, which is fairly common. I wouldn't want to fluster her before the procedure, either."

"Procedure?" Reina repeated in an uncertain tone. "What exactly are you going to do to her, doctor? What is this procedure?"

"Perhaps that was an inappropriate term. Hypnotherapy is the use of *hypnosis* as a healing technique. It is primarily used to help people with emotional and psychological issues. It might not be useful for everyone, though. So, I need to know a little more about Julie."

"Um, okay... What do you need to know?"

"Well, has Julie had any past health issues?"

Reina shrugged and said, "She's been sick here and there, but she hasn't had any serious medical issues. I mean, the girl hasn't been to an actual hospital since she was born."

"Good, good. Now, is there a history of mental illness in your family, Ms. Knight, or the family of Julie's father?"

Reina took a deep breath as she stared down at her high heels. She didn't enjoy speaking about Julie's father. She wanted to bury that part of her life.

She said, "No. No, I don't believe there is."

Morris nodded and said, "Good. And, is there any history of substance abuse in the family? Or, for that matter, any substance use at all? Do any of you drink? Do you smoke?"

"Before his death, Julie's father had some problems with substance abuse. He was an alcoholic. He moved on to marijuana, then heroin, then cocaine... He used *a lot* of drugs, doctor. This was after Julie was born. It was even after Nick was born."

"Does Julie have any problems with drugs?"

"I think... Listen, I know she smokes marijuana and a boy she calls her 'boyfriend' messes with other drugs. I honestly don't believe she's done anything more than some weed. She hasn't done any drugs in the past week, either. I know that for a fact."

Morris clasped his hands together in front of his chest, he smiled and he said, "Okay. I think I've heard enough. You can wait out here or go to the seating area. This is confidential, though, so you won't be allowed inside and the door will be locked. I'll see you in a moment, ma'am."

Despite her doubt, Reina smiled and said, "Thank you, doctor."

***

Morris entered his small office. He closed and locked the door behind him, then he turned his attention to the center of the room.

Julie lay on a chaise lounge chair—an elegant upholstered sofa. She nervously smiled at the doctor. The chair was comfortable, the doctor was pleasant, but she still felt anxious. As her mother explained, she hadn't been to a hospital since she was born. She had a few physical exams throughout her lifetime, but she skipped more of them than she attended.

Morris sat in a wingback chair in front of the teenager. A table with a candle sat between the doctor and the patient. As the doctor crossed his legs and smiled, Julie turned her attention to a corner in the room—the corner behind Morris.

The corner was unusually dark. Sunshine poured through the window and lamps illuminated the room, but the corner was *still* dark. She could see the faint silhouette of a person in the darkness, too—a shadow within the shadows.

Julie thought: *are we alone or did it follow me here?*

Breaking the silence, Morris asked, "What are you looking at, Julie?" Julie clenched her jaw and shook her head. Morris smiled and said, "That's okay. You don't have to tell me now. As I was telling you earlier, I'd like to try hypnotherapy on you. I believe this will help us find what's bothering you. It'll help us find the source of your... *anxiety,* for want of a better word."

Julie asked, "So, you're just going to hypnotize me

or something? What's going to happen to me?"

"Well, it won't be like anything you've probably seen on television. It's rather simple, really. Trust me, I won't make you cluck like a chicken or speak a different language or anything like that. I am going to attempt to make you focus while trying to make you as comfortable as possible in order to extract information from you. Specifically, I will attempt to extract things you may have forgotten. Please remember, I won't be forcing you to do anything against your will. Just follow my directions and let it happen naturally. Okay?"

"Okay."

As he stood from his seat, Morris said, "I want you to take slow, deep breaths." He walked to each lamp in the room and turned off the lights. As he closed the blinds and pulled the curtains together, he said, "Remember, this is a safe place. You are in control, Julie. I am here to make sure you stay in control."

Julie squirmed in her seat and glanced every which way as darkness enveloped the room. She breathed deeply through her nose, trying her best to keep her composure. She felt the sweat dripping across her neck and brow, she felt her heart beating in her throat.

Morris sat down in the wingback chair. He ignited a lighter, then he lit the candle on the table. The flickering flame offered enough light to illuminate the doctor and the patient. The light, minuscule compared to the room, also comforted Julie.

Morris said, "I want you to focus on this flame. Don't look at me, don't look at the darkness, only look at the flame. When the candle goes out, the hypnosis will end." He leaned back in his seat, hiding his face in the darkness. He said, "Relax, Julie. Concentrate on nothing but the flame."

Despite her skepticism, Julie concentrated on the candle. She gazed at the fire, watching as the flame undulated like a belly dancer. Her breathing and her heart rate slowed. The sweat on her face started drying on her skin. For the first time in days, she felt calm.

Morris realized Julie had entered a relaxed state—an altered state. He seized the opportunity to find the source of her anxiety.

He asked, "Are you comfortable, Julie?"

In a monotonous tone, Julie responded, "Yes."

"Good, good. You are in an altered state within a controlled environment. There is nothing to worry about. You are safe and you know this. Do you understand me?"

"Yes."

"Julie, I want to talk about your fears. Let's start with something simple: what scared you as a child?"

"Bullies. Roller coasters. Spiders. Clowns. The bogeyman."

"Those are very common fears, Julie. Tell me: did you ever overcome those fears?"

"Yes, I... No. No, I'm lying. I didn't overcome them."

Morris tilted his head, curious. He asked, "What are you still scared of?"

Absently staring at the flame, Julie responded, "The bogeyman."

"I see. Do you believe the bogeyman is real?"

"Yes."

"Okay. Can you tell me about the bogeyman? Is he... Is he a bad person? Does he hurt you?"

"Yes."

"Did the bogeyman attack you last week?"

Julie kept her eyes glued to the flame. The side of her mouth and her eyelids twitched. The silence in the room was unnerving. She wanted to scream, but the words were clogged in her throat—silencing her, *suffocating her.*

Julie stuttered, "Y–Yes."

"Do you know him? Do you recognize the bogeyman?"

"I–I'm... I'm not sure."

His elbows on his knees, Morris leaned forward until his face was illuminated by the candle. He smiled—a gentle, understanding smile. He didn't want to distract his patient, he solely sought to make her comfortable as she faced her demons.

Morris said, "I want you to try to remember the bogeyman. I want you to tell me about him. I want you to imagine him in this room with us. What does he look like?"

Teary-eyed, Julie grimaced and responded, "I'm scared. I don't want to see him."

"Remember, Julie, you're in a safe space now. You're in a bubble. You can see him, but he can't see you."

The light from the fire inexplicably weakened. Yet again, Morris' face was swallowed by the darkness, but he didn't seem to notice. Motionless, he sat and patiently waited for Julie's response.

Despite the unusual circumstances, Julie didn't take her eyes off the flame. She blinked, causing tears to stream across her cheeks.

From the corner of her eye, she watched as the ominous figure emerged from its corner. The humanoid figure crept behind the doctor and slowly approached the flame's ring of illumination. It moved with eerie convulsions, its limbs and head twitching with sudden irregular movements. The figure leaned over the wingback chair, but the doctor didn't notice it.

Julie still refused to take her eyes off the flame. For the first time since encountering the bizarre entity, she stood her ground. The flame on the light grew stronger again, whisking the shadows away while revealing Morris and the figure.

Julie could finally see the figure's face. It was the man from the diner. The curly-haired, brown-eyed, lean-bodied man stared at her with a blank expression. She could also see his sweaty, nude body from the corner of her eye. She was startled by his nudity, but, at that moment, she finally recognized him. She put a name to the face.

She knew the bogeyman—and the bogeyman knew her.

A lump in her throat, Julie croaked, "I know him. Oh, God, I know him..."

Morris, unaware of the entity's presence behind him, asked, "You can see him in this room now?"

Focused on the candlelight, Julie said, "Yes."

"And you recognize him?"

"Yes."

"Who is he, Julie? Who is the bogeyman?"

Julie gritted her teeth, then she said, "He's a monster. He's an evil monster. No, no, no. He's worse than that. He's an evil bastard. He's... He's my father."

She shook her head and squirmed back in her seat as the entity walked around the wingback chair and approached the candle. The man—Richard Knight, *her father*—moved with wavering motions. He twitched and trembled, jittery like a child who consumed too much sugar. His movements were unnatural, demonic and horrific.

He opened his mouth as wide as humanly possible, then he moaned. The moan of agony was slow and loud, but Morris didn't hear it.

Julie frowned and shook her head, terrified. She couldn't stay focused on the flame. Her eyes cycled between the candle and her father as the entity slowly approached her. Her heart raced in her chest, beating faster as her father neared her seat. Although the doctor didn't see or hear the entity, he could see the fear in his patient's wandering eyes.

Concerned, Morris said, "Julie, focus on the flame. Remember, you're safe here. He can't get you. You only have to focus on the light."

"He's coming for me... He's coming. Please, don't let him get me. I don't–"

Julie stopped talking as her father stopped moving. The pair stared at each other. It was as if the rest of the world were whisked away. It wasn't a pleasant reunion, though. Before she could sigh in relief, she felt some fingertips on both of her cheeks. Someone was caressing her face from behind, touching her gently.

She frantically swiped at her face and wiggled on her seat as she cried, "Don't touch me, daddy! I don't want you to touch me! Stop! Stop it! Why won't you stop?!"

"Julie, look at the light!" Morris shouted. "He can't hurt you here! Look at the light!"

Julie stopped her frantic movements and gazed at the flickering flame, tears gushing from her eyes. As soon as she locked eyes with the fire, Morris blew out the candle. With that, the malevolent figure vanished. Julie could no longer feel the fingers on her face, either. The nightmare ended.

***

Sunshine entered the office through the window while the lamps illuminated every corner of the room. The malevolent aura in the office vanished.

Julie sniffled and shuddered as she sat in the chaise lounge chair, holding a handkerchief to her nose. She was terrified by the surreal experience, but she found some relief through the treatment. She found some much needed closure.

Morris smiled as he sat in his wingback chair, blatantly satisfied with the hypnotherapy. As far as he was concerned, the treatment was a success. Silent and attentive, he carefully examined his patient's condition. To his relief, she was fine.

Morris said, "I have an assessment. It's not overly detailed, but it may help you understand the situation. Would you like to hear it?"

"Y-Yes..."

"I think it's safe to say: the bogeyman is your father. Is that correct?"

Julie stared vacantly at the floor as she contemplated the doctor's theory. She never consciously thought of her father as the bogeyman, but, deep down, she knew the truth. It made sense to her, so she nodded.

Morris asked, "Did your father abuse you, Julie?"

Julie looked up at Morris. The question steamrolled her like a tank. It was a heavy, personal question that wasn't easy to answer for anyone.

In a cracking voice, Julie stuttered, "H-He... I didn't really think about it before now. I... I never thought about it since it happened, actually. He, um... He touched me, you know? He–He molested me when I was eight, maybe nine years old. He touched everything, he put his fingers into... *everything.*" She grimaced and shook her head, fighting the urge to weep. She said, "I just could never believe he would do that to me. He was *so* good before he started drinking. He used to take me to the park every weekend and push me on the swings. I rode my first roller coaster with him and it was... it was fun. He gave me this *beautiful* toy bear when I was six. It was the best toy I ever got—the cutest, most lovable bear. I still keep it in a shoe-box under my bed."

She rubbed her eyes with her palms as tears streamed down her rosy cheeks. She needed a second to recompose herself. The bittersweet memories were tarnished by her father's despicable actions.

She said, "I still can't believe it. I didn't want to remember what he did to me, I only wanted to remember the... the good stuff. Why did I block it all? Why did I do this to myself?"

Morris responded, "You did this because you needed help. You did nothing wrong, Julie. I believe what is happening to you now—the visions of sexual assault—is because of your past abuse. You may have never thought about it, but the memories of abuse were always lingering in your subconscious. They're free now and that may be what has been causing these violent, ghost-like episodes."

"Why?"

"Why? 'Why,' what?"

"Why is this happening now? What did I do to deserve this?"

Morris gazed into Julie's bloodshot eyes,

disappointed. He wanted to give her all of the answers, but he wasn't even finished asking all of his questions. He wouldn't be able to give her a rational explanation until she received more treatment.

Opting for a simple answer, Morris said, "There was a trigger. At least, that appears to be the most likely reason. Something might have happened to you in the past few weeks that caused you to subconsciously remember your father or your abuse—or both. This could have been a mention of your father or even the mere mention of abuse on a soap opera or movie."

"I don't know. I... I can't think of anything. I'm sorry."

"There's no need to apologize, Julie. We can find the trigger together. In the meantime, I don't want you to stress about it. We've made a lot of progress today—more than I ever anticipated. I want you to know that you are *okay.* You are not sick, you are not guilty. We'll get through this together and we'll accomplish even more in the near-future."

Julie couldn't help but smile as she listened to the doctor. He made her feel comfortable. However, a few words echoed through her mind: *you are not sick.* She couldn't tell if he was serious or if he was just trying to make her feel better.

She asked, "Will I need medicine?"

"I don't believe medication is necessary now, but I won't cross anything off my list. If it comes to it, I'll recommend an amazing psychiatrist. We'll take care of you. You have my word."

"Thank you, doctor. Thank you for everything."

Morris smiled and nodded, then he said, "It's my pleasure, Julie. I'm going to go into the hall now. I'm going to speak to your mother about the procedure, then, if you'd like, I'll bring her in so we can discuss our findings. Is that okay?"

"That's fine."

Julie watched as Morris exited the room. Despite the closed door and thick walls, she could hear her mother's muffled voice. *She heard me screaming and crying,* the teenager thought, *she probably knows about everything already.* She turned her attention to the corner of the room. The darkness still lingered, but it looked normal. The figure was gone, too.

Julie sighed and stared down at herself. She was saddened by the memories of abuse, but she felt like everything was going to be okay. A burden was lifted from her shoulders. The shackles around her wrists and ankles were broken.

She was finally free.

Chapter Seven

Back to Normal

Three weeks had passed since Julie visited Dr. Morris for her first appointment. Since then, she had met the good doctor two other times, visiting him on a weekly basis. She made progress, learning about herself and the effects of sexual abuse on the human mind, but she didn't experience another powerful outburst. The distorted figure of her father didn't haunt her again.

Julie stood in her mother's bedroom. She stared at her reflection on a full-body mirror, fixing her hair and adjusting her makeup. She appeared healthier than before. Her eyes were vibrant and her skin was soft. She was well-rested. She still struggled with anxiety here and there, but, most of the time, she was able to control her stress.

As she stared at her reflection, Julie whispered, "Everything is okay. I'm fine, I'm safe. I can... I can move on with my life. No, no. I *have* to move on with my life. There's nothing to be scared of. The bogeyman is... dead."

She rubbed her lips together and shoved her hair behind her ear, then she nodded in determination— she was ready. She walked out of the bedroom, her bag slung over her shoulder. She walked down the hall until she stopped at her bedroom. The room called her name, inviting her with honeyed words. Those nonexistent words were enough to convince her to take a peek.

She pushed the door open, then she leaned on the doorway and gazed into the room. She hadn't slept in her own room since the night of the second attack. Instead, she spent her nights in the master bedroom or in the living room.

The room was normal, though. Everything was exactly as she left it. It didn't feel malevolent, either, but she was still frightened. Although she had started to convince herself that none of it happened, she still felt like she was raped in that room.

The experience scarred her because it felt so real. She felt like a real victim of rape. The room would have to be redesigned in order for her to return to it comfortably.

From the doorway to his room, Nick said, "Julie."

Julie glanced over at her brother. She smiled, happy to see him. The boy didn't look happy, he was clearly tormented by the situation, but he still brought a smile to her face. She admired his strength in the face of adversity. He didn't cry or complain to his mother, he didn't complicate the situation for his family. He was a trooper.

Julie asked, "What's up, squirt?"

"I was just, um... I don't know, I was wondering if you were okay. Are... Are you okay?"

"Thanks for your concern, kiddo, but... Don't worry about me, alright? I've been feeling a lot better."

"If you need anything, you can just ask me. I can run to the store for you when mom isn't around or... or anything like that. Just ask and I'll do it, seriously."

Julie simpered and nodded, then she said, "Thanks for the offer. I really appreciate it. Is there something else you wanted to tell me, Nick?"

Nick opened his mouth to speak, but he stopped

himself before he could utter a word. He wanted to talk to his sister about *that* night—the night she was attacked in front of her family. He wanted to tell her about what he saw: an invisible person standing up from her bed. He couldn't muster the courage to confess, though. His sister was doing better, he could clearly see that, so he didn't want to interfere with her progress.

He sighed, then he said, "Nah. I just wanted to see how you were doing. Do you... Do you want to watch a movie or play a game or something?"

"Not tonight, squirt. I've got a job to do. Sorry."

"That's okay. I was just wondering. I'll see you later."

"Yeah, I'll see you around."

Julie walked away from her room as her brother retreated to his own bedroom. She stopped at the living room and stared at the sofa. She noticed her mother wasn't stressing about their finances. Instead, Reina rested on her side on the couch and watched television.

Julie asked, "Are you taking the night off? *Finally?*"

Reina glanced back at her daughter and said, "Yeah. I still have some work to do, but... it can wait, you know?"

She furrowed her brow as she examined her daughter's appearance. Julie wore a loose gray shirt, blue jeans, and white sneakers. Her hair was tied in a ponytail, too. She wasn't dressed for a big date, but she wore more than her usual pajamas, which she had been wearing around the house ever since the attack.

Reina asked, "Why are you dressed up? Are you going somewhere?"

Julie clasped her hands in front of her stomach and said, "Yeah. I took a job babysitting the Turners' kid, Sue. It should be easy."

Reina sat up on the sofa and stared at her daughter with wide, worried eyes. She blinked erratically and shrugged, struggling to conjure the words to respond.

She stuttered, "A–Are you sure about this? Do you... Do you really want to do that? I think it's too much stress for you, hun."

"I'll be fine. Dr. Morris said I should start getting myself out there so that's what I'm doing. I'm ready to start working again, mom. Mrs. Turner said Sue is easy to babysit anyway. It's not a big deal, really."

"It sounds like a big deal to me, baby. You don't know what can trigger your... 'your condition.' I don't feel comfortable letting you go. I just... I can't, okay? I don't want you to get hurt. Stay home and, in a few weeks, maybe you can go back to work at the diner. At least Tracy can take care of you there. Okay?"

Julie smiled and shook her head. Most teenagers despised overprotective parents, but she could feel the love in her mother's voice. Reina wasn't trying to stop Julie from enjoying her life, she was just trying to make sure she had a life to enjoy.

Julie said, "I've been feeling better lately. I'm not just saying that, either. I can breathe without feeling that lump in my throat. I can talk about dad without feeling ashamed. I can walk without, um... staggering. I'm feeling better and I want to keep making progress." She looked around the living room with glittering eyes, as if she were reminiscing about something. She said, "I need to get out of this house, too. I love it here, but I have to spread my wings again.

I need to... to go places that aren't the doctor's office or my house. I need some fresh air—some freedom."

Reina puckered her lips and inhaled deeply through her nose. Her eyes glistened with tears, but she refused to cry in front of Julie. She wasn't ashamed of showing weakness, though. She only wanted to match her daughter's strength—to stand by her with unwavering determination.

Reina said, "Okay, okay. The Turners, um... They live a few blocks away, right?"

"Yeah, I'm going to walk over there right now. It's, like, a five-minute walk."

"Okay. Make sure your phone is charged and call me at the first sign of trouble. I'm serious, Julie. Call me if you need *anything.* I'll even babysit the kid for you if I have to. Okay?"

Julie giggled, then she said, "Okay, okay. I'll be back in three, maybe four hours. Love you, mom."

"I love you, too. Be careful, baby!"

Julie walked out of the house. She stopped on the porch as the afternoon sunshine beat down on her soft face. The warm sunshine caressed her body, filling her with a sense of reassurance. With her head up high, she proudly marched down the porch steps and headed to the Turner house, ready to resume her normal life.

Chapter Eight

Babysitting

Julie sat in the living room of the Turner house, leaning on the armrest of a three-seat sofa. Across from the sofa, a flat-screen television played a muted movie about a possessed girl—edited for television, of course. She could hear Sue Turner playing in her bedroom, having a tea party with dolls and stuffed animals.

Julie held her cell phone to her ear, humming softly as she listened to her boyfriend. Daniel spoke about looking for work while Julie was away.

Daniel said, "Yeah. That's all I've been up to. I've really been trying to better myself, babe. It sounds cheesy, but I... I actually thought I lost you."

Julie responded, "I told you: I was never going to leave you. It wasn't about you. I wish I could have called, but... things just got a little crazy and I didn't have the time."

"Yeah, I get it. It's just... I kept thinking: *why isn't she answering? Why won't she take my calls? Who is she with?*"

Julie huffed and rolled her eyes, then she smiled and said, "I wasn't with anyone, Daniel."

"I know, I know. But, I mean, I know you said you didn't have time, but it's been, like, three weeks since the last time we talked. You couldn't find *one* minute to call me? Shit, a text would have been cool, too. What happened to you?"

"It's a long story. It's a lot longer than you could

ever imagine. I was... I was just sick."

Julie didn't enjoy lying to her boyfriend, but she couldn't reveal the truth. She was barely learning how to deal with her past abuse, she couldn't willingly invite more people to witness the spectacle. Besides, she rationalized it as a white lie—*a half-truth.* She was seeing a doctor after all, so she was technically sick.

Daniel asked, "Was it serious? What kind of sickness could knock you out for three weeks?"

As she twirled her hair and stared at the television, Julie responded, "It was serious, but I don't feel sick anymore. I'm feeling better these days. I'm still going to need some time to heal, but I'm getting there."

"That's good, that's real good," Daniel said. His words were followed by an unusual moment of silence. He snickered, then he said, "You know, I must have spent hours jacking off every day while you were gone. Don't worry, though. I thought about *you* while I was looking at *them.*"

He chuckled at his playful joke, teasing his girlfriend about his 'sexual escapades.' Julie laughed, too, but she knew where the conversation was headed.

Daniel said, "I'd like to spend some 'quality' time with you later, Jules. We can have a romantic night. I'll take care of you, you take care of me. What do you think?"

A romantic night—Julie sighed and rolled her eyes upon hearing those words. Although he tried to act playful, veiling his intentions with candied words, her boyfriend's intentions were clear.

Julie said, "All you think about is sex. You'd think you were a virgin in some shitty teenage comedy, but we both know that's not true. You'd screw a hole on the ground if the mud looked like a girl, and you can't act anyway."

Daniel said, "I'm sorry, babe. I was joking. You know me, I have a big mouth... and a big dick."

"Well, you have one of those..."

Daniel chuckled, then he said, "I guess I don't have such a big mouth after all." The pair shared a laugh—just like old times. Daniel said, "Seriously, though, we should hang out soon. We can smoke, we can drink, we can... We can do whatever you want."

"No. No, I'm not smoking or drinking right now, Daniel. I just... I can't."

"Why not? Is it, like, because you're sick or something?"

"No, I'm just not messing with any of that right now."

"You sure? I've got the dankest bud around."

Before the pair could start talking about drugs, the sound of a *creaky* floorboard emerged in the living room. Julie lowered the phone and glanced over her shoulder.

Sue Turner, a five-year-old blonde girl, stood in the hallway. Her hands clasped behind her back, the girl smiled and twisted her hips as she watched her babysitter. She appeared mischievous, as if she had just set the house on fire, but she wasn't a troublemaker.

Julie lifted the phone up to her ear and said, "Daniel, I have a little visitor. I'm going to have to call you back later. Bye."

"Alright, I'll talk to you later, babe."

Julie shoved the phone into her bag, then she turned her attention to the child. The girls stared at each other, grinning like devious children participating in a prank war.

Julie asked, "Well, what do you need, sweetie? I told you already: I'm not very good at tea parties. I get drunk on tea and start fighting with everyone. You don't want to see that."

Sue giggled, then she said, "It's time for my bath. I always take a bath before I go to sleep. *Always.*"

"Okay, go ahead and take a bath, then I'll tuck you in."

"I can't. I'm not allowed to take one by myself. You have to watch me, remember?"

"Oh, you want me to watch you..."

Julie bit her bottom lip and looked around the living room. The request was innocent: Sue's parents didn't want their daughter to have an accident in the bathroom and they trusted Julie to watch over her in the tub. However, Julie didn't feel comfortable in the situation. The idea of helping Sue bathe felt wrong. Despite the water and soap, it made her feel filthy because of her past memories of abuse.

Trying to keep a smile on her face, Julie asked, "Would it be okay if you took a bath in your bathing suit?"

Sue shrugged and said, "Okay. It's like going to the pool!"

"Yeah, exactly. Go put on your bathing suit and I'll meet you in the bathroom in five minutes. Okay? Go, go, go."

Sue giggled as she pranced to her bedroom, blissfully unaware of the demon's haunting her babysitter. Julie smiled as she watched her, reassured by the child's innocence.

***

Her Suffering   73

Julie sat on her knees beside the bathtub and stared vacantly at the rippling water. She occasionally splashed some water on Sue, trying to keep a semblance of normality. Sue, wearing a pink one-piece bathing suit, played with a toy boat and a rubber whale. She happily hummed as she splashed in the warm water.

Julie smiled as she watched her. Although she was skeptical, she felt safe around the child. She believed the girl was truly pure. She hoped her wicked thoughts would vanish thanks to Sue's presence. She thought: *good always trumps evil, right?*

The babysitter glanced around the small room, a reminiscent look on her face. The bathtub-shower combo was directly in front of her. Behind her, there was a toilet, a sink, and a medicine cabinet. To her right, the open doorway led to the master bedroom. They used the bathroom connected to the master bedroom because it was the only bathroom with a tub in the house.

As she dunked the rubber whale into the water, Sue asked, "Are you going to sneak your boyfriend here after I sleep?"

Julie giggled, then she asked, "What in the world are you talking about?"

"My last babysitter got fired because her boyfriend came over. Mommy and daddy caught them in the living room kissing and stuff. It was funny, but mommy was *so* mad. She screamed and she kicked them out and *fired* her. I was a little sad. I liked her. She was nice."

"Well, she shouldn't have done that. It's okay to talk on the phone and rent movies and all of that junk, but, as babysitters, we're supposed to be watching you. That's all."

"Yeah, but... if you bring your boyfriend, I won't tell. I'm not a tattletale like the other girls. I'm... I'm a big girl."

Grinning from ear-to-ear, Julie responded, "Oh, *really?* That's good to know. It's okay to tell every once in a while, though. It even makes you a 'bigger' girl, too. My brother tells on me, but it's to help me. If you think something's wrong, just tell. Alright?"

Sue sighed, then she said, "Okay." The room became quiet for fifteen seconds. Sue smirked and said, "You can bring your boyfriend and I can stay up an hour later to eat ice cream. Deal?"

Julie laughed. Like her boyfriend, the young girl had hidden intentions. However, Sue's plans were much more innocent. Julie and Sue giggled together, sharing a genuine laugh.

As she recomposed herself, Julie said, "I'll tell you what: if you promise not to tell your mom, I'll stay up with you and we can–"

The water splashed at the foot of the bathtub, causing a wave to ripple towards Sue's back. The soapy water spilled over the edge of the tub, cascading across its side and dripping onto the linoleum tile flooring. It appeared as if someone had stepped into the bathtub—but only Julie and Sue were inside of the room.

Pale-faced, Julie gazed at the water at the end of the tub. The water stopped rippling and returned to normal. Sue also stared at the foot of the tub. She glanced over at her babysitter, looking for an answer to the inexplicable.

As she stared at the water, searching for any other anomalies, Julie stuttered, "D–Did you... Did you see that, Sue?"

"Yeah. I saw it. The–The water moved," Sue responded. The young girl's breathing intensified as she felt the raw fear in her babysitter's heart. Teary-eyed, Sue asked, "What happened, Julie? Did... Did someone come in with me? Is... Is someone here?"

Julie heard Sue's questions, but she couldn't respond. She didn't have the answers and she was dumbstruck by her first response. *She saw it and she felt it,* she thought, *if it's him, then it wasn't in my head.* Part of her felt relieved to know she wasn't insane. However, her relief could not match the overwhelming fear the entity's presence brought to her body.

Julie said, "I think bath time is over. Come on, sweetie, let's–"

The water rippled again, moving towards the girls as if someone had taken a step forward in the bathtub. There was something in the room with them.

Before she could utter another word, Julie felt a strange sensation in her body. She felt as if her internal organs were twisting and turning. Vomit clogging her throat, she felt nauseous and dizzy as the room spun frantically around her. She tightly closed her eyes with each blink, struggling to cope with the pain in her head.

She gasped as she slowly levitated from the floor. She could see her feet dangling over the edge of the bathtub, she could see the shocked expression on Sue's face.

Julie whispered, "Not again..."

The incorporeal entity hurled her at the wall above the bathtub. Julie screamed as she flew over the tub. She grunted as she hit the tile wall. She felt a sharp pain across her ribs and shoulder. Then, she fell into the water. Her head missed Sue's body by an inch.

Sue, baffled by the event, climbed out of the bathtub—a wave of water following behind her. She slipped and slid across the flooded floor until she reached the doorway, then she turned around and stared back into the bathroom. Sobbing and shuddering uncontrollably, she helplessly watched as her babysitter struggled to escape from the tub.

What could a child do during such a terrifying event?

Julie couldn't lift her head out of the water. She flailed her limbs every which way, but to no avail. She felt a powerful grip on the back of her neck. It looked as if someone—or something—was trying to drown her in the bathwater. She clearly screamed and struggled under the water. Her words couldn't be heard, but the water churned and bubbled.

As soon as the grip loosened on her neck, she lifted her head out of the water and gasped for air. Weakened by the near-suffocation, she stumbled out of the bathtub—practically *dragging* herself out. Her sopping wet clothes felt heavier than before and water dripped from her soaked hair. Disoriented, she turned her attention to the door.

Sue still stood in the doorway, seemingly paralyzed by her fear. Rosy-cheeked, the child watched the attack as if she were watching a horror movie for the first time. She couldn't comprehend the situation, but she couldn't look away, either.

Julie shouted, "Run! Run, Sue! Go... Go to your room! *Run!*"

As she staggered to her feet, she felt a gut-churning sensation in her body again. She levitated from the floor, her feet dangling half-a-meter from the ground. She was thrown towards the wall above the sink. Her head crashed into the mirror on the medicine cabinet. The glass shattered and a large gash formed on the side of her head.

Sue shrieked upon witnessing the brutal assault. Julie fell to the floor, semi-conscious. Shards of sparkling glass were trapped in her cut, amplifying the pain. Blood streamed across her face and dripped into her eyes. Her vision was blurred by the attack and reddened by the blood. She could still see into the master bedroom, though.

She watched as Sue ran out of the room. She listened until she heard the sound of Sue's door closing. She was scared of the malevolent spirit and she knew what was coming, but she was relieved by the sound of the door closing. *She shouldn't see this,* she thought, *no girl should ever have to feel or see this.*

She closed her eyes and lowered her head until her lips kissed the floor. She whimpered as her pants and underwear slid down her legs. Yet again, she was violently penetrated by the entity. She clenched her jaw and cried, but she refused to scream. She didn't want to attract Sue back to the bathroom with a bloodcurdling shriek.

She just accepted the attack, counting each thrust until the inevitable end.

Chapter Nine

The Hospital

Reina rushed through the sliding doors and slid to a stop in the emergency room. Nick stopped behind his mother. Reina wore a bathrobe over her nightgown while Nick wore his flannel pajamas. They didn't care about their outfits, though. They were only concerned with Julie's well-being.

Reina rushed to the reception desk. She slammed her fist on the desk, capturing the attention of everyone in the room. Paige Garcia, the registrar, hopped and stepped back, startled by the woman's aggressive approach. She held her hands up in a peaceful gesture—*calm down, everything's okay.*

Reina said, "I... I got a call that my–my daughter was taken to the emergency room. Her name is Julie Knight. Okay? *Julie Knight.* Where is she? Is she okay?"

"You're Julie's mother?" Paige responded in an uncertain tone. "Okay. Well, I'm going to have a nurse walk you up to her room in a minute. I just need–"

"Is she okay? Is my daughter okay?"

"I'm sorry, I can't answer that question for her. I'm not her doctor, but if you give me a minute–"

"Is she okay?!"

"Ma'am, please calm down."

"Oh, God," Reina muttered as her legs wobbled. She was disoriented by the pessimistic thoughts of her daughter's health. She said, "She's alive... She's alive, right?"

Paige rapidly nodded and said, "Yes, yes. Look, she's in stable condition. I just can't give you a *full* report on her health." She glanced back and said, "Jen, call Dr. Coleman."

Breathing heavily, Reina bent over near the counter. She whimpered, tears dripping from her eyes and plopping on the floor. Nick tightly grabbed her robe, trying to stop himself from crying. He wanted to be the man of the house after all.

"Reina," a soft feminine voice said from behind them.

Reina stood straight and wiped the tears from her cheeks, then she turned around. She found herself staring into the small seating area behind her. She only recognized three people: *the Turners.* Rob, a proud husband and father, remained seated. He offered a nod and half-a-smile. Kathy, an equally proud mother and wife, and Sue stood behind Reina and Nick.

Reina stuttered, "K–Kathy... It–It's been a while." She looked over at Sue and said, "Hi, Sue. I haven't seen you since you were a baby. You've grown up so fast."

Sue slinked behind her mother. From the outside looking in, she looked bashful. She was actually upset because of the incident in the bathroom, though.

Kathy said, "Reina, I'm sorry."

Reina asked, "What happened to Julie? Is my baby okay? Please tell me she's okay... *Please.*"

"I really don't know. I know she was hurt, there was some sort of accident at home, but... I just don't understand what happened."

"What? What do you mean?"

Reina glanced down at Sue, hoping the young girl

would reveal the truth. Sue stared back at her, peeking from around her mother's leg. Although he remained quiet, Nick recognized the look in the girl's eyes—it was the look of fear.

Kathy said, "I'm sorry, Reina. She's not talking to anyone. No one is talking to anyone. Sue didn't have anything to say to the police or the doctors and your daughter didn't want to say anything, either. I have no idea what's going on. I hope everything's okay. Please don't blame us for this. Don't hate me. I can't–"

"Ms. Knight," a strong, deep voice interrupted them, along with the sound of *clicking* footsteps. A doctor approached the group. The man said, "My name is Elijah Coleman. I was treating your daughter earlier. Don't worry, she's conscious and stable. Will you take a walk with me?"

"S–Sure."

Coleman nodded at Nick and the Turners, then he said, "I think it would be best if the rest of you waited here in the seating area."

Reina patted Nick's head and said, "Wait with Mrs. Turner, okay? You heard him, right? Your sister is okay. Just wait here. I'll be back."

Coleman and Reina walked through a set of doors. The couple walked down a wide corridor, strolling past patient rooms, offices, and closets.

As they walked, Coleman said, "Julie is not gravely injured. We may have to keep her here for a few nights to run some tests, but I think she'll ultimately be fine. My biggest worry right now is an injury to her head. We've treated the wound, but she may have a concussion. So, I may prescribe some medication for headache pain and possibly some anti-nausea medication. We'll see."

"What happened to her?"

As the pair turned into another corridor, Coleman pointed ahead and said, "This is her room up here." He beckoned to the police officer standing in front of room 1031. The doctor said, "I've been told that you've met Officer Connor Stone already."

Reina stared at the officer in disbelief. She recognized him from the night of Julie's attack. *It happened again,* she thought, *he's going to try to take my baby away, isn't he?*

Connor said, "Hello, Ms. Knight. I wish we were meeting under better circumstances."

Reina asked, "Can we please get to the point? What happened to Julie?"

"Well, let me tell you what I've been told. Little Sue told me Julie was watching her bathe, then Julie... Julie apparently started 'floating' for a second, which caused her to fall into the bathtub. After she climbed out, she apparently fell again and smashed her head on the medicine cabinet."

"F–Floating?"

"*Floating.* That's the word she used. It's most likely a product of a child's overactive imagination. She refused to clarify afterward, though. She just stopped talking. Regardless, the doctor and I agree: she fell and smashed her head on the medicine cabinet. The floor was wet, so she probably took a nasty tumble."

Reina nodded in agreement. Sue's story was outlandish while the cop's theory was realistic. However, the officer's mere presence at the hospital concerned her.

She asked, "If she just fell, if she's okay, what are you doing here?"

"The initial call was of an *attack.* I was in the area

and I arrived with my partner. We found Julie, barely conscious and soaked. She had crawled into the master bedroom. Sue called it in as an attack, she spoke about her babysitter being hurt by *something*, but, like I said, she might have simply slipped. Maybe not. We don't know."

"Well, what did Julie say? Why are you only telling me about a five-year-old's story? What did my daughter say?"

Connor sighed, then he explained, "Julie has refused to cooperate—*again.* She claims she fell, too, but there may be more to it."

Chiming-in, Coleman said, "I think it would help if you spoke to her, Ms. Knight. She'd feel more comfortable with you and we're willing to give you the room for complete privacy. We just want to make sure she gets the help she needs."

Reina stared at the door. The silence in the room was daunting. She was afraid of seeing her daughter, too. She nodded in agreement, though.

She said, "Okay, I'll... I'll talk to her."

***

Reina slinked into the room with her head down, closing the door behind her. She planted her forehead on the door and took a deep breath, mentally preparing herself for her inevitable encounter with her daughter. She was not fond of hospitals, so her nosocomephobia was only aggravated by her daughter's visit to the emergency room.

She turned and gazed into the room. Her eyes immediately watered. Her legs wobbled and her arms trembled as she drew a long, shuddery breath. She staggered towards the center of the small room.

Julie lay on a hospital bed with her eyes closed,

draped in a blue gown. Her head was wrapped in a bandage. The bandage was clean, the bleeding from the wound underneath was controlled, but the side of her head still appeared swollen and bruised. Her arm was also bruised, green and purple, but it wasn't broken during the attack.

Although they hadn't yet shared a word, Reina knew it was more than a tumble in the bathroom. Her mother's intuition told her that her daughter was viciously attacked. She felt the warning before, but she failed to stop her daughter from leaving the house. She couldn't help but blame herself. She sat at the edge of the bed, sniveling.

Julie opened her eyes. Upon spotting her mother, she grimaced and cried. Reina nodded, speaking without saying a word—*yes, mommy's here for you.* She leaned forward and hugged her daughter.

Reina asked, "What happened, sweetie?" She leaned away from her daughter and caressed her cheek. She said, "They told me you fell in the bathroom. What really happened?"

Julie looked away from her mother. She tried to stop herself from sobbing since she knew the doctor and the cop were waiting for them outside. *If I say I was raped again, they'll think I'm crazy,* she thought.

Julie said, "I fell... I slipped and I fell."

Reina grabbed her chin and gently pulled Julie's head, forcing her to stare into her eyes. She said, "It's okay. It's just me. No one can hear us." She nervously smiled and giggled, then she said, "I'm not wearing a wire or anything like that, baby. I'm just here to help. Tell me: *what happened?*"

"I... I... I fell. Can't you just believe that and leave me alone? God, why can't everyone just leave me alone?"

Although her words weren't meant to be malicious, Reina was heartbroken by the response. She frowned and whimpered as she leaned closer to her daughter. She placed her chin on her daughter's head and brought her face closer to her chest, trying her best to comfort Julie during such a stressful time.

Her voice cracking, Reina said, "This is my fault... I've wanted to say that to you for so long. I wish I saw the signs, I wish I could have stopped that bastard from... from touching you, from mo-*molesting* you, from..." She stopped as a lump formed in her throat. She loudly swallowed and coughed, then she said, "He's dead now, but I... I just want him to come back so I can kill him. This is all my fault, Julie. I'm sorry, baby. I'm so sorry."

Julie, unable to control herself, buried her face in her mother's bosom and cried. She tightly grabbed the back of her mother's robe as she finally released the venomous depression she tried to bury in her body for so long. She grunted and groaned, tears streaming down her rosy cheeks and mucus dribbling onto her lips.

The pair pulled away from each other. Reina kissed her daughter's forehead as Julie stared down at her lap and sniffled.

Julie said, "Mom, I'll tell you the truth, but you have to promise you won't tell them out there. I don't want to stay in the hospital, I don't want to talk to the police anymore. I just want to go home."

Reina looked at her daughter with a raised brow. The request was simple, but she feared she would be hurting her daughter by honoring it.

Julie said, "You have to promise me. Okay? And, if you break that promise, I will *never* forgive you... for anything. Promise me, mom."

Reina nodded and said, "Okay, baby. I promise: I won't tell them a word and I'll take you home. Okay? You have my word on that. Now, talk to me. What happened at that house?"

Julie gazed into her mother's eyes—she trusted her. She turned and stared vacantly at the empty space on the wall across from the bed.

Teary-eyed, she said, "It... It happened again. The same thing that happened in my room happened while I was watching Sue in the bathroom. I didn't see anyone, though. It grabbed me and it threw me around the room. Then, it... it pulled my pants off and–and it... it raped me. It was just like last time, but it somehow followed me to their house." She paused to breathe, trying to stay calm. She swiped at her nose and said, "After it finished, I pulled my pants up and I crawled onto their bed. I couldn't do anything else. I just felt so weak and pathetic."

"No, no, no. No, baby, you're not weak. You're strong. You hear me?"

Julie nodded and said, "It doesn't matter. It raped me, but I don't want them to know that. I don't want to get checked by the doctors. I'm scared. I mean, if it actually happened, then some... some... some *ghost* is raping me. If it didn't happen, then I'm just going crazy and they'll send me to some mental hospital. I just want to go home, mom."

Reina caught a glimpse of the dread clinging to her daughter's eyes. She glanced back at the door and thought about calling for help.

Julie grabbed her mother's hand and said, "You promised."

Reina sucked her lips into her mouth and nodded.

She said, "I know, I know. We... We're going to stick with the same story, okay? The floor was wet and you fell. I'm going to go out there and tell them to leave you alone. I'm going to bring you home as soon as possible."

"Thank you. I... I love you so much."

"I love you, too, sweetie. You sit tight and wait for me here. I'll be right back. I'll see if I can bring Nick in here, too."

Julie watched as her mother marched out of the room. She could hear the conversation in the hallway from her bed. It was muffled, but she could hear enough. Her mother claimed Julie fell in the bathroom and Sue's version of the event was distorted due to a scary movie they watched earlier in the evening—Reina kept her promise.

As she listened to her mother's voice, Julie smiled, sniffled, and whispered, "Thank you so much, mom... Thank you."

Chapter Ten

The Suffering

Reina stood in the kitchen, staring vacantly at a stock pot on the stove. The sound of the stove hissing and the soup bubbling echoed through the otherwise quiet house. She wasn't home alone, but she felt like she was abandoned by the world. *A woman and her soup*—it was the loneliest story she could imagine.

It had been a week since the incident at the Turner house. Traumatized by the event but refusing medical attention, Julie was brought home. Reina hid her daughter's secret and vowed to protect her from the entity—an entity whose existence was debatable. Nick agreed to help around the house, dealing with the housework while staying out of trouble in school.

Reina's trance was broken by the sound of a bubbly ringtone. She glanced over at the countertop. Her phone vibrated on the counter, moving an inch with each tone. The name on the screen read: *Timothy McGuire.* Timothy was her direct superior—*the boss.*

Reina sighed, then she whispered, "What the hell do you want, Tim?" She shook her head as she swiped her finger across the screen. She answered, "Hello, this is Julie Knight."

"Reina," Timothy said, his voice deep and raspy. "Where are you? I thought you were coming in today."

"No, I never said I was coming in. I told you: I need time off."

"Yes, and we gave you time off. We've been giving

you time off for the past month. We've been trying to work with you. Hell, Reina, we even gave you work to do from home. We're treating you like a damn student, but you're not doing your homework. You're just not working. How do you expect us to pay you if you don't work? Huh? How?"

"I don't expect anything from anyone. Look, I'll *try* to come in next week. If my—"

"Next week? We're busy *now,* Reina. I know you're trying to take care of your daughter, but... Christ, she's a grown woman. She can take care of herself. Leave some soup in the fridge, give her some sleeping pills, then go about your day. You don't have to coddle her like some sort of baby."

Reina scowled and cocked her head back, astonished by her boss' offensive response. He didn't understand her family's issues. He acted as if he could fix a broken bone with a bandage. In a sense, it was funny. The man wasn't married and he didn't have children, but he still handed out parenting advice like a student passing out fliers on a college campus. She couldn't tolerate his crap anymore.

She said, "Listen to me, *Timmy.* I'm done with your bullshit. We're going through something tough right now and I don't need you to add more fuel to this damn fire. You can fill out your own paperwork, you can make your own damn coffee. Go ahead and fire me 'cause I'm *not* abandoning my daughter."

"Calm down, Reina. I'm just looking out for you and your career. You don't want to—"

"I don't want a career with you or your company. I quit, you selfish bastard."

She disconnected from the call, then she tossed the phone on the counter. She dug her fingers into her hair as she stared at her cell phone. She expected it to ring again, but Timothy didn't call back. Reina thought: *what have I done?*

"Is everything okay?" Nick asked from the archway between the living room and kitchen.

Reina glanced back at her son. She was haunted by her daughter's condition, she regretted her words during the call, but she remained strong. Even without a job, she cracked a smile and nodded at her son, as if to say: *everything's fine and dandy.*

Reina said, "I'm okay, Nick. We're okay. I just had a little argument with my boss. It doesn't look like I'll be stressing about work for a while. Well, I won't have to worry about *going* to work, getting a new job is a different issue. What I'm saying is... You should go to your room. Play some video games and forget about this. Everything's okay."

As his mother fiddled with the knobs on the stove, Nick asked, "What about Julie? Is she okay?"

"She... She's still sick, sweetheart. She's getting better, though," Reina said as she looked into a cupboard. She retrieved a bed tray and a bowl. As she poured the soup into the bowl, Reina said, "I know it's scary right now, but you have to stay strong. As long as we're strong, she'll stay strong. She hasn't had any... any 'fits' since she got home, right? Well, that's because we're taking care of her."

"But, she won't come out of her room..."

Reina placed the bowl on the tray, then she placed the ladle beside the stove. She looked over at her son, her eyes narrowed in a curious manner. The boy was perceptive—she couldn't fool him.

She explained, "Julie needs time and support. Things are happening to her that we just can't understand. Just... Just stay strong for her, okay? Keep her in your thoughts and everything will be fine. Now, go to your room and try to relax. I don't want you to stress about this. You're just a kid, Nick. Let me take care of this."

Nick lowered his head and said, "Okay. I guess I'll see you later..."

"I love you, sweetheart."

"Love you, too," Nick said as he walked away from the kitchen.

***

Reina pushed Julie's door open with a swing of her hips. She squinted as she stood in the doorway, balancing a bowl of hot soup on a bed tray. The bright light in the bedroom caused her to hesitate while her vision blurred.

The room was illuminated with dazzling fairy lights, which were pinned onto the walls. Lamps from the other bedrooms and the living room were also moved into Julie's room to help brighten the darkest corners. The area under the bed was even illuminated by an old night-light.

Julie sat in bed, her back against the headboard and her knees up to her chest. Since arriving from the hospital, she did not experience any new attacks. Yet, she was perpetually frightened and vigilant. Due to the surreal nature of the attacks, she felt like she couldn't trust anyone—including herself.

She wore pink flannel pajamas—a button-up top and loose pants. She wore the same clothes for an entire week and she refused to bathe. She would call her mother to her bedroom with a bucket whenever she needed to relieve herself.

Black bags hung under her bloodshot eyes due to

her lack of sleep. Her cheeks and nose were rosy since she couldn't stop herself from crying. Her hair was tied in a messy bun, strands protruding every which way. She didn't care about her appearance, though. She was solely concerned with surviving the increasingly aggressive attacks.

Reina sat at the edge of the bed and placed the tray on the nightstand, then she gently pushed down on Julie's knees. Julie gasped and squirmed upon feeling her mother's hands. She looked scared and surprised, as if she hadn't noticed her mother's presence until that moment. She calmed herself as soon as she recognized Reina, though.

Reina placed the bed tray over Julie's lap. She stroked her daughter's forehead, shoving the stray hairs aside. She hated seeing her daughter in such a distraught state.

She said, "I brought you some soup, princess. Come on, let's eat." Julie constantly glanced at every corner of the room, as if she were hearing someone call her name. Reina asked, "Are you feeling okay? Hmm? Aren't you hungry, baby? Please, just eat a little. It's good for you."

Yet again, Julie did not respond. She continued to look at every corner of the room. She was lost in her thoughts—controlled by her fear.

Reina sniffled, then she said, "I can't believe this is happening to us. What's wrong, baby? What can I do to help you?" She stared down at her trembling hands and whispered, "What am I saying? I couldn't help you then, I can't help you now. I'm sorry, Julie. This is my fault. It's all my fault... I was such a fool. I should have never trusted him."

Upon hearing her mother's cries, Julie tightly

closed her eyes and shook her head, trying to snap out of her fear-induced trance. She stared at Reina with a set of puffy eyes, saddened by her mother's self-loathing. She didn't blame her for her problems. She chose to bury her father's abuse without telling her mother. She blamed herself more than anyone else.

Julie said, "I'm sorry, mom. I just...I can't concentrate. I'm scared. Like, I'm scared of *everything.* I feel like I'm seeing things everywhere. Just when I think I'm safe, I see something else at the corner of my eye. It's scary. It's so scary..." She sniffled and swiped at her pink nose, struggling to keep her composure. As she stared vacantly at the wall above her computer, she said, "I don't know if I believe in it, I never really thought of it before, but I feel like I'm being pulled into the... the pits of hell. I don't have a fever, I'm not sick, but I feel like I'm burning inside. Do you know what it's like to feel like that? Have you ever felt that *burning* feeling inside of you?"

Reina said, "Of course. I've felt it when I was younger and I've been feeling it a lot recently. It's... It was guilt. I felt guilty and I feel it now."

"Should I feel guilty for what he did?"

Reina narrowed her eyes and shook her head, caught off guard by the question. She said, "No, sweetie. You shouldn't feel guilty for that. What your father did, that's *his* sin. You are the victim, not the... the perpetrator. No matter what you think, you didn't make it happen. If anything, I should feel guilty for missing it. I should have known."

"It's not your fault, mom. I was a kid... I just didn't know what to do."

"It's not your fault, either, Julie. It's... It's Richard's

fault. Come here," Reina said.

She moved the tray to the nightstand, then she grabbed her daughter's head and pulled her closer to her chest. The pair cried as they shared a warm hug.

Reina said, "We have to stop blaming ourselves. We can't bury the past and pretend like it never happened, but we have to move forward. I promise, I'll be with you every step of the way. I'll never let you go. Never."

Julie groaned as she cried. She agreed with her mother, but she couldn't find the words to respond. So, she just nodded and sobbed. They reached a wordless understanding.

***

A smile blossomed on Reina's face as she hugged her daughter. She rocked her in her arms and gently shushed her, acting as if she were taking care of a crying baby. Julie found some relief in her mother's bosom. She felt like a child again. And, at that moment, she wasn't afraid of the bogeyman.

While the pair embraced, a light bulb above the computer exploded. The sound of glass shattering—bursting into a dozen small shards—interrupted the sweet mother-daughter moment. The glass landed on the desk, sprinkled on top of the keyboard like salt on a pretzel.

Reina and Julie stared at the broken bulb with wide eyes. Reina looked at the broken bulb, then down at the desk. She struggled to connect the pieces. Julie kept her eyes locked on the broken bulb and the dark space it left behind. The small circle of darkness between the other fairy lights was daunting. It was enough to open the doors to hell.

Teary-eyed, Julie stuttered, "D–Do you see it?"

Reina inhaled deeply—a long, shuddery breath. She nodded and said, "Yes, it... it must have been an old bulb. These lights are very old, Julie. We've had them since you were a kid. I'll replace it soon, okay? Don't worry, it's–"

"Not the bulb. The... The man in the room."

Reina froze with fear. She slowly turned towards her daughter. She could see Julie wasn't lying. She wasn't playing a prank, she wasn't trying to lighten the mood. Her daughter actually saw someone else in the room—*a man.*

Reina looked around and searched for the intruder. She couldn't see anyone, though. Aside from the darkness created by the broken bulb, the room remained the same—in appearance, at least. She felt a cold draft. By simply staring at the dark spot on the wall, she felt an evil presence in the room. The darkness was terrifying.

Julie wiggled out of her mother's arms, wheezing and shuddering. She slipped and slid on the mattress until her back hit the headboard.

She cried, "No! No, don't come near me! Get away from me, you sick bastard! Please stop!"

Reina stuttered, "Wha–What are you–"

She tumbled off the bed as Julie spun around and flew two meters into the air, her back scraping the ceiling. She watched as Julie landed face-first on the bed with a loud *thump* sound. The air was knocked out of her due to the sudden fall. Julie breathed noisily as she squirmed on the bed and gazed at her mother with dim, hollow eyes.

Horrified, Reina teetered back until she clashed with the wall near the door. She helplessly watched as her daughter's pants were pulled down. She could see Julie was wearing three pairs of underwear. It was a futile attempt at preventing future attacks. Before her very eyes, the panties were ripped from her daughter's body with ease. The garments were thrown to the floor.

In a raspy tone, Julie said, "Mom, help..."

Her bottom lip quivering, Reina stuttered, "Wha-What's happening? I-I don't see anyone, sweetie..."

As she felt a phallic object penetrating her vagina, Julie cried, "Mom! Help me!"

"Leave her alone!" Reina barked at the empty space above the bed.

Reina ran forward with her fists overhead, ready to swing at the invisible intruder. As soon as she reached the bed, she felt a strong grip on her chest. She was pushed back by a powerful force, knocking her off her feet and hurling her back at the wall near the door. She grunted as she crashed into the wall, then she coughed and moaned as she slid down to the floor.

She thought: *what pushed me? Who's hurting my baby? How do I stop this?!*

Dazed by the attack, Reina watched as the entity raped her daughter. Her ass up like a dog playing with her owner, Julie's head was pinned to a pillow and her back was arched. The entire bed violently shook under her as the entity thrust into her. She cried at the top of her lungs, veins protruding from her neck and brow, but to no avail—the attack didn't end.

She felt a hand on her stomach, but she couldn't see it. Before she knew it, she was flipped over onto her back. Her limbs were spread away from her body. She felt hands on her wrists and ankles, as if a group of people were holding her down, then she felt the penetration again. The entity continued to rape her in the missionary position.

A minute felt like a lifetime. The headboard hit the wall with a loud *thud*, then the bed stopped moving. The entity finished defiling Julie's body.

Holding her hand up to her chest, Reina stood up and took a step closer to the bed. She was suspicious of the silence. Julie, ravaged by the malevolent presence, turned her head and stared at her mother. She croaked and groaned, unable to say a word.

Julie trembled on the bed. Her eyes rolled up into her head. A croaking sound emerged from her throat as her mouth widened. It sounded as if she were having trouble breathing.

Teeth chattering, Reina approached the bed and stuttered, "Wha–What's wrong, sweetie? Oh, God..."

She reached into her robe pocket, then she stopped—she forgot her cell phone in the kitchen. She believed her daughter was having a seizure. She needed to call 911, but she was afraid of leaving her daughter alone.

As Reina took a step back, preparing to run out to grab her phone, Julie smirked and giggled. Without breaking eye contact with her mother, she slowly slid her hand across her bare stomach, gently gliding her fingertips across her skin. She stopped at her crotch, then she started masturbating. She thrust her hips as she vigorously rubbed her clitoris. She moaned and giggled as she pleasured herself in front of her mother.

Reina was at a loss for words. She couldn't think of a single appropriate response to the situation. *'Stop masturbating, it's not natural.'* She was experiencing the impossible for the first time in her life, so she didn't have a response prepared for such a bizarre event.

As the young woman masturbated, the bed began to tremble violently. The bedposts swayed left and right and the floorboards screeched under the furniture. The lights in the room flickered. The light grew stronger, then weaker, then stronger again.

In a raspy, guttural tone, Julie sternly said, *"She's mine."*

The door swung open. Nick stepped into the doorway and gasped, shocked by his discovery. He was surprised by his sister's actions and horrified by the shaking bed. As she masturbated, Julie glanced over at her brother and licked her lips, then she flicked her tongue at him. The deviance glimmering in her eyes was obvious. She was not herself.

Noticing Julie's lecherous behavior, Reina ran towards the door and covered her son's view. She pushed him into the hallway, then she reluctantly closed the door. She couldn't comprehend the situation. She couldn't help her daughter with Nick in the room, either. She needed a professional.

Chapter Eleven

A Doctor's Visit

Dr. Alexander Morris climbed out of his car, carefully closing the door behind him. A leather medical bag in his right hand, he walked up to the front gate and stared at the small house. Perhaps it was the overcast sky above him or maybe it was the hysterical call that summoned him to the home, but he felt a foreboding atmosphere looming over the house.

The good doctor shrugged it off as the jitters—*nothing to worry about.* He marched up the walkway and up the porch, then he knocked on the front door. As if she were waiting on the other side, Reina opened the door before Morris could even lower his hand. The pair shared a silent, awkward gaze.

Morris said, "Good evening, Ms. Knight. I came as fast as I could. How's Julie?"

Trembling uncontrollably, Reina responded, "She's not well, doctor." She stepped aside and beckoned to him. She said, "Come in. Please, hurry."

Morris glanced around the home as he walked into the living room. He puckered his lips and stared down the hall. Nick stared at him from his bedroom doorway. As the doctor smiled and waved, the boy retreated to his bedroom.

Morris said, "Your son seems shy."

Reina stared at him with a worried expression. She didn't have time for small talk.

Morris said, "Sorry. What's the problem? You were quite... *emotional* on the phone. Did she have another panic attack?"

Reina held her trembling hands up to her chest and shook her head. She indistinctly mumbled, struggling to reveal the truth. Her mind was flooded with pessimistic thoughts. She feared she would lose Julie and Nick if she revealed what she saw. *A capable guardian*—she had to keep that facade afloat. *He'd think I'm crazy if I told him the truth,* she thought, *I can't let him tear us apart.*

Morris smiled tenderly and said, "It's okay, Ms. Knight. I'm here to help in any way possible. What's wrong? What happened to Julie?"

"She... Well, she had another 'fit.' It was another... *attack,* like the one she told you about. It's difficult to explain."

"It's okay. Take your time."

Reina took a deep breath, trying to tame her anxiety. She said, "It's a little different from the last attack. She just hasn't been the same. It's strange."

"Strange?" Morris repeated with a pinch of doubt in his voice. "What exactly has she been doing?"

"Well, she... she's been throwing herself on the bed—*hard.* It looked like it was impossible, I wouldn't have believed it if I didn't see it, but she's just throwing herself higher and harder than ever before. She also... Oh, God, this sounds so crazy, but she said something in a different voice. You understand what I'm saying? She spoke to me with a deep voice—a *nasty* voice. I've never heard her speak like that before."

"What did she say?"

"She said, 'She's mine.' I have no idea what she was talking about, though. I'm... I'm sorry."

Reina lowered her head and stared at the floor. She

decided to keep the details about the powerful shove and Julie's masturbation to herself.

She said, "Please, doctor, hypnotize her again. It helped so much last time. Please, help my baby. I just want to see her happy again. I just... I can't deal with this anymore. It's too much. Hypnotize her and make this go away."

Morris watched as Reina cried. He could see she was sincere. He patted her shoulders and tried his best to comfort her.

He said, "I'll see what I can do. It might not be a good idea to hypnotize her if she's in a deranged state, though. Hypnosis can be dangerous for people with mental health issues. Now, I'm not saying she's mentally ill, but it might be better if we avoided any potential triggers. I will talk to her, though, and I'll try my best to get to the bottom of this. Where is her room?"

"The second door on the right."

"Okay. Wait for me here. I'll be back in a moment."

The doctor marched down the hall, his head held high. He was confident, unperturbed by Reina's horror story. He had seen it all before—or so he thought.

As she watched him from the living room, Reina whispered, "Please save her..."

***

Morris stepped into the bedroom, quietly closing the door behind him. He furrowed his brow as he examined the room. The fairy lights nailed to the walls caught him off guard. The broken bulbs were also worrisome. Since Reina left the room, ten other bulbs exploded. So, several spots in the room were dark. The corners of the room were the darkest, though.

The doctor rubbed the nape of his neck and took a step forward. He was confused by the set-up of the lights, but he was more concerned about Julie's inexplicable absence. The young woman didn't lay on her bed or sit at her desk. She had vanished without a trace.

Morris asked, "Julie, are you in here?" There was no response. He chuckled, then he asked, "Are you playing a game? Is it hide-and-seek? Hmm? Well, let's see where you're hiding..."

He stepped forward, floorboards creaking under his dress shoes. He checked the most obvious place—under the bed. He knelt down and tossed the dangling covers onto the mattress.

As expected, Julie rested under the bed in the fetal position. She didn't appear frightened, though. She held her hand to her mouth and simpered like a misbehaving child. Morris extended his arm forward, as if he were reaching for a handshake. He smiled—a warm, sincere smile—and nodded at her, trying his best to create a safe environment for the girl.

He said, "Come on. Let's get you into bed, little lady."

In a squeaky voice, Julie blushed and said, "Okie-dokie."

Julie grabbed his hand and crawled out from under the bed. Morris covered his eyes and looked away upon spotting her bare bottom half.

As she sat on the bed, Julie asked, "What's the matter, doc? You've never seen an eighteen-year-old's pussy before? It's exciting, isn't it?"

"Please cover yourself up. We have to talk."

"Okay, okay... Calm down. It's not like it bites,

doctor."

Julie giggled and tossed a blanket over her legs. She pulled the blanket up to her chest and wiggled on the bed, searching for the most comfortable position. Morris dragged the computer chair up to the foot of the bed and sat down. He placed his medical bag on the floor beside him.

The doctor said, "Julie, your mother tells me you've been having some issues lately. She told me you were 'attacked,' like before. How are you feeling right now?"

In her normal voice, Julie shrugged and said, "I'm okay, I guess. I mean, everyone has problems, right? So, I had a little outburst. Big deal. That's no reason to call a doctor, right? I'm okay, really. Anyway, how are *you* doing, doc? Is everything fine with the wife?"

Morris nervously smiled and said, "Everything is fine. Thank you for asking. Now, I can't help but feel like there's something wrong here. I'm not calling you a liar, I would never do that, but I do think you're hiding something."

He crossed his legs and leaned back in his seat as he carefully analyzed Julie's condition. She seemed normal at the moment, but there was something off about her. He considered all of his options. A formal interview seemed to be his best bet, but he couldn't fully trust his patient.

Julie asked, "Doctor, are you going to hypnotize me?"

"I could do that, sure. It would have to be justified, though."

"I think you can justify it. You're a doctor after all. People trust you. You wouldn't be here if my mom didn't trust you. So, I think you should hypnotize me.

It would be nice. Put me under your spell and... and *molest* me."

Morris rolled back on the chair, shocked by the vulgar suggestion. He had spoken to Julie several times since her first reported attack and she never behaved in such a lewd manner.

Julie said, "I think it would be easy—*very easy*—to assault a young girl while she was hypnotized. And, that girl might like it. Right?"

Sweat dripping across his brow, Morris indistinctly mumbled. While the doctor struggled to speak, Julie tossed the blanket aside and opened her legs wide, revealing her bare crotch. Morris gasped and rolled farther back on his chair. He opened his mouth to speak, but he could only utter the croak of a word—*oh, ah, um.*

As she casually rubbed her clitoris, Julie asked, "What's the matter, doctor? Haven't you ever thought about fucking one of your patients? One of your young, innocent patients?" She spread her vulva and said, "Just look at this tight, pink pussy. Doesn't it look appetizing? It's beautiful, isn't it? I love it, doctor. You'll love it, too."

Morris grabbed his bag and stood from his seat. He wiped the sweat from his brow and walked to the door with his head down, refusing to even spare a glance for his patient. As he reached the door, the lock turned on its own. He twisted and jiggled the knob, but to no avail. He was trapped in the bedroom.

Morris asked, "What's going on here? How are you doing this?"

Without stopping her masturbation, Julie moaned and responded, "Me? It's not me, doctor. It's just a sticky lock. It does it on its own sometimes. Now, sit down. I'm not done with you."

"I should—"

"*Sit down!*" Julie shouted, her voice deep and raspy.

Morris leaned on the wall, startled by his patient's voice. He stared at Julie with narrowed eyes, cycling through years' worth of experience in an attempt to find an advantage against her. Julie smirked and twitched as she giggled, pleased. She let out a loud moan as she slipped two fingers into her vagina.

In a hoarse tone, she said, "Come here, doctor. I want you to fuck me. Yeah, I want you to fuck me *so* hard. It would feel so good, wouldn't it? It would feel just like when daddy did it. No, no, no. It would feel better because you're a doctor. You know my tight little pussy better than I do. Oh, please come here and take care of me, doctor." She loudly moaned as her head swayed. In a soft tone, like a child's voice, Julie said, "Rape us, rape us. Please, fill my little pussy with your cum. You know you want to..."

Morris was at a loss for words. He slowly opened his bag and took a step forward. He didn't want to alarm Julie, but he feared she was losing the battle against herself. At heart, although he was frightened, he knew he had to step in and help her.

Before he could take another step, Julie glanced over at Morris. Eyes brimming with tears, she grimaced and shook her head. She didn't stop masturbating—she *couldn't* stop—but she was clearly herself. The pain in her eyes was evident.

In her own voice, Julie said, "Help me. I—I can't stop it. Please, help me. I want to... I just want to die. I want this to end. I..." She stopped, then she pulled her hands away from her crotch. She glared at Morris and said, "I want to die."

She dug four of her fingernails into the top of her forearm, right below the crook of her elbow. Her fingernails penetrated her skin. Blood streamed every which way, soaking her arm. She gritted her teeth as she scratched downward to her wrist. The sound of her skin ripping resembled the sound of paper *shredding.* She was trying to slit her wrists vertically.

Morris rushed forward and pushed her arm away. A geyser of blood squirted from her arm and nearly struck his face. He placed his body over her chest, trying to stop her from harming herself as he reached into his bag. He pulled a needle—a prepared sedative—out of his bag. Despite Julie's kicking and screaming, he was able to inject her arm.

He continued to restrain her while trying to soothe her emotional pain. The process was slow. An intramuscular sedative could take minutes to take effect. He waited with her, though. One, two, three... *ten minutes*—he waited ten minutes until Julie fell unconscious.

***

Morris and Reina sat in the living room. Two mugs brimming with coffee sat on the glass table in front of them. The television—for the first time ever, it would appear—was off. The home was eerily silent. Video games couldn't be heard from Nick's bedroom, weeping couldn't be heard from Julie's room.

Reina stared at the doctor, anxiously waiting for his assessment. From his incessant foot-tapping to his trembling fingers, she could see he was rattled by the experience.

Reina said, "You haven't said a word since you came out of her room. Julie is quiet now, but... What happened in there? Is she okay?"

Morris sighed, then he said, "I had to... sedate your daughter, Ms. Knight. I gave her something that would keep her calm for a few hours. I also bandaged the wounds on her arm. I don't believe she's in any immediate danger, but she should go to a hospital as soon as possible. She may need stitches."

"Wounds? Stitches? What are you talking about?"

"While I was in the room, Julie began to exhibit erratic and violent behavior. She tried to cut her wrist with her fingernails."

"Is it bad? The cuts?"

"Like I said: she'll live, but she should go see a doctor as soon as possible."

Reina, unnerved by the revelation, nodded in agreement. Morris grabbed the mug and took a sip of his coffee.

The doctor said, "I am more concerned with Julie's mental health than the wounds on her arm. She should be evaluated by a group of professionals. She may be showing signs of early onset schizophrenia or other personality disorders."

"What? No, no. I told you: there is no history of mental illness in our family."

"I'm not saying it is certain. Okay? If schizophrenia could be diagnosed through a checklist, I probably would have taken the gamble and guessed that she was schizophrenic. However, mental illness is much more complex. She needs to be monitored carefully by a group of professionals for an extended period."

Reina stared down at her lap and repeated, "Schizophrenia..." Her eyes widened as she remembered Julie's leap—the girl nearly touched the ceiling. She said, "It can't just be schizophrenia. I've seen her *fly* across the room, Dr. Morris. I've heard her voice change."

"I've heard her voice, too, and it's not completely unbelievable. I've studied cases like this before. And, her sudden surges in strength may be linked to seizures or muscular spasms."

"Muscular spasms? No, doctor, that's just not possible. I'm saying she *flew* into the air. I saw it."

"I'm not saying you didn't see her 'fly.' You must understand: muscular spasms of this magnitude can make it appear like your daughter has... has superpowers. Of course, she really doesn't, but she's just using all of her energy at once. On top of that, such a traumatic experience can lead to... false memories. You saw something happen, but it might not have been *exactly* what you remember."

Reina didn't believe him. She could sense a trace of doubt in his voice, too. She didn't question him, though. He was a doctor after all and he had the ability to diagnose her. Morris took another sip of his coffee, trying to act normal around the distraught mother.

The doctor grabbed Reina's hand and said, "I know this is difficult to hear, but you must listen, Ms. Knight. Your daughter's health is at risk. Her mind may be deteriorating as we speak. We must take Julie to a mental health facility and she must be evaluated. You might not want to hear this, either, but I have the legal authority to have her committed."

Reina glared at Morris and responded, "Excuse me? You have to be joking? What gives you the right? Huh? Who do you think you are?"

"She harmed herself in front of me, ma'am. She is a danger to herself and others."

"No, no. That's not right. She... She didn't harm herself until *you* showed up. You went into the room and you locked yourself in there. I heard the moaning out here. My son probably heard it, too. You could have done something to provoke her. Don't tell me you have the 'legal authority' to do anything to my daughter 'cause I have the legal authority to sue you, too."

Morris lifted his hands up in a peaceful gesture. He said, "Nothing inappropriate happened inside of your daughter's room. Okay? She said it herself: the lock on the door is sticky. And, you said it, too: she's been acting erratically. Moaning is not out of the ordinary for a victim of abuse who is in a 'deranged' state. I'm not trying to hurt you or your daughter. I'm trying to do the opposite. You know that very well."

Reina leaned back in her seat and dug her fingers into her hair. The doctor's compassionate plea came off as a threat to her loved ones. She refused to lose her daughter and separate her family. Bug-eyed, she stared at the mug on the table. She imagined herself smashing the mug on the doctor's head. She would go even further than that to defend her family, too.

Teary-eyed, she said, "You can't do this. You came here to help us, not to fill your own pockets. Please, just help us. Give us something to work with."

"I don't have any other options left, Ms. Knight."

"Let me keep her at home for a little longer. She can fight through this, can't she? Sending her to a hospital, locking her up like some sick animal... That can hurt her, can't it?"

Morris could feel the pain in Reina's voice. Truth be told, he didn't fully understand Julie's condition. He didn't know if a psychological evaluation would actually help her. He only knew it would stop her from harming herself and her family.

He said, "Here's what I can do for you: I won't have her committed." As Reina sighed in relief, Morris explained, "*But,* I want to check up on her once or twice a week here at your home. If I believe her mental condition is worsening, I will have her committed—with or without your consent. Understood?"

Reina swallowed the lump in her throat, then she said, "Understood."

As the doctor babbled about the conditions of their compromise, Reina glanced over her shoulder and stared down the hall. She could only think about Julie's health. She thought: *am I making the right choice or am I being a selfish mother?* She didn't have an answer. She could only hope for the best.

Chapter Twelve

The Other Options

Reina sat in the living room, her fingertips gliding across the trackpad on her laptop. Eyes full of tears, she scrolled through the transactions on her bank account. Her checking account had dropped to triple-digits—barely sitting above six-hundred dollars. Her savings were completely exhausted, too. Without a job, she was out of money.

How could a single mother take care of her family without cash? In a world dominated by money, it was nearly impossible to support oneself, let alone a family.

Reina knew how to manage her finances. She had raised her kids by herself for nearly a decade. She didn't know how to deal with significant health issues, though. She didn't know how to manage the consequential bills, either. So, she wasn't certain if she'd be able to take care of her daughter. *Can I leave her at a mental health hospital without paying? Is that the right thing to do?*–she thought.

Her fingers trembled over the keyboard as she sniffled. The idea of failing to take care of her daughter debilitated her. She was more horrified by the idea of losing Julie, though. She didn't know what it was like to be in a mental hospital. Regardless, she made a promise to keep her daughter out and she planned on keeping it.

From behind the couch, Nick said, "Mom..."

Reina hopped in her seat, startled by her son's soft

voice. She glanced back at Nick, then she turned away. She wiped the tears from her cheeks with her robe as she closed the tab on the web browser. She didn't want him to see her tears or her empty bank account.

As she rubbed her eyes, Reina asked, "What is it, baby? Everything okay?"

"I was... I just wanted to talk, I guess."

"About what?"

Nick did not respond. He leaned over the couch and stared at the laptop, blatantly lost in his thoughts. Reina turned towards her son. She pushed the hair away from his brow, then she gently massaged his cheek.

She said, "You need a haircut. Sorry, we've just been really busy lately, haven't we? You must feel neglected, right? I'm so sorry, hun."

Nick responded, "It's not that. I know why you're busy. I was just wondering: what happens next with... with Julie?"

"Well, the doctor is convinced that there is something wrong with Julie's brain. You understand? He thinks it's a psychological issue. We agreed to give her some time before we... we take other steps."

"Psychological? Like, it's all in her head?"

Reina closed her eyes and nodded.

Nick shrugged and said, "But, didn't you tell them you saw it? She didn't do that by herself, right? You saw it, didn't you?"

Reina responded, "I don't know what I saw, but... you're right. I saw something that was impossible. I couldn't say anything, though. Do you know what they'd do to me if I said I saw her flying up to the ceiling by herself? Or if I told them about... about everything else? They'd send me in for a mental

Her Suffering 115

evaluation, then our family would be split up. They'd think I couldn't take care of you and your sister. God, this is all my fault..."

Nick sighed in disappointment. At the same time, he felt some relief. He wasn't aware of the consequences of telling the truth. When the doctor arrived, he wanted to run down the hall and tell him *everything* about the events in Julie's bedroom. If he did, he could have caused his family to split up—according to his mother, at least.

Nick said, "Mom, you're not crazy. Julie's not crazy, either."

"What? What are you talking about, Nick?"

"If you're crazy, then so am I. I heard Julie's voice change. And, the first time it happened here, I saw the bed move. It looked like someone was getting up, but there was no one there. I couldn't see him or her or... or it. We can't all be imagining the same thing, right? We can't all be crazy, *right?*"

Reina was baffled by the confession. She turned and stared at her laptop, speechless. Nick sat down beside his mother. He stared at the laptop, too. They each shared the same idea, but they waited for the other to say it out loud.

Nick said, "I don't really know what's happening to Julie, but I think I have an idea. Can I show you something?"

Reina pointed at the computer and stuttered, "Wha-What? On the-the laptop?

"Yeah."

"O-Okay."

As he typed, Nick said, "There's this group online that, um... that hunts ghosts and spirits and stuff. I know it sounds stupid, but I think they're the real deal."

Reina laughed and shook her head, trying to shrug off the suggestion. Children had wild imaginations after all. Yet, she couldn't deny the fact that she was interested. She didn't believe in ghosts, but she felt like an answer to Julie's problems lurked beyond the human realm.

Nick said, "Everything doesn't have to have a 'real' explanation. You know, there are some questions even my Science teacher can't answer. I mean, no one *really* knows what happens after we die, right?"

Reina frowned and lowered her head. *It all goes black*—she stopped herself from uttering those words. She didn't want to frighten Nick and she didn't actually know what happened after death.

Nick pointed at the screen and said, "Look."

Reina leaned forward and examined the site. Nick led her to a website titled: *Unearthly Happenings.* Although the speakers were muted, a video played on the homepage. The video depicted a young crimson-haired woman walking through a dilapidated house. She appeared to be talking at the ceiling—trying to talk to spirits. Unearthly Happenings was clearly a web-show about ghost hunters.

Reina asked, "Are they... Are they real? Do you think they actually do their job? You think they can talk to spirits?"

Nick responded, "I think so. I've seen all of their stuff and it all looks real, especially compared to all of the fake crap–" He paused and bit his bottom lip—his mother didn't like it when he cursed. He said, "I think it's real. That girl, her name is Rose Love. She's a... a... a medium. But she doesn't have a bunch of producers faking everything for her like the ones on TV. She only works with a guy called Edmund Kowalski. He's like the cameraman and the tech-guy."

"Okay. And... I can contact them? They'll talk to me? I mean, I'm not saying I believe all of this, but, um... You really think they'll be willing to help us, Nick?"

Nick glided his fingers across the trackpad. As he cycled through a few pages, he said, "They work with anyone if they think it's real. I don't know if they charge, but you can talk to them here." He moved the laptop and showed the screen to his mother. He said, "You can call them on Skype and video-chat with 'em."

Reina spotted the 'Contact me' button on the website. She justified her urge to call by pretending it was a favor for her son—she was humoring him to make him feel better. At heart, the group caught her attention and she believed they could help. She tapped the trackpad, then she muttered to herself—*damn.*

She said, "It's busy... I'll call them later, though, sweetie. Just go to your room and relax, okay?" As Nick walked down the hall, Reina shouted, "*Nick!*"

Nick glanced back with a furrowed brow, as if to say: *what is it?*

Reina said, "Thank you for being so brave. Call me if you need anything."

Nick nodded at his mother, then he strolled into his room. Reina waited in the living room by her lonesome, constantly checking on the Unearthly Happenings hotline. One minute snowballed into thirty. Then, the call connected. She wiggled on her seat, adjusted her hair, and cracked a smile as she found herself staring at the host of the show—*Rose Love.*

Rose was a red-haired woman who glowed with wondrous youth. She couldn't have been older than her twenties. Her milky white skin was soft and smooth. Her blue eyes sparkled like the ocean on a sunny day. She wore a casual sleeveless maxi dress, which molded to her curves perfectly. She gave off a caring aura, too.

Rose smiled and said, "Hello, ma'am. I assume you're calling about a serious inquiry. Well, I hope so. I've dealt with enough fake calls for one day."

Reina responded, "It's serious. This is... This is very serious and urgent. I'm calling from, um, Southern California to–to get your help."

"Okay, good. I mean, it must *not* be good if you're calling for serious help, but well, we get a lot of prank callers and it's good that... Never mind. My name is Rose Love. My partner-slash-financer, Edmund Kowalski, is currently running an errand. He usually deals with this sort of stuff, but I'm happy to help with any of your problems. So... what can I help you with?"

My daughter is possessed by the devil—she thought about blurting out the response. It seemed too straightforward, though.

Eyes glistening with tears, Reina explained, "My... My name is Reina Knight. My daughter's name is Julie Knight. She's a sweet teenage girl. She's made a few mistakes in her life, she makes bad dating decisions, but she's a good person. She's also in trouble. I don't know how to explain what's happening. I can only tell you what she's told me and what I've seen. This isn't a prank, okay? This is my daughter's life we're talking about."

Rose, captivated by Reina's speech, asked, "What's

happening to your daughter, ma'am?"

"My daughter has been... suffering. She says that she is being raped by someone she can't see. Except, sometimes she can see him... and he looks like her father... *and,* her father's dead. I haven't seen a ghost, not like the ones in the movies, but I've seen things. I've seen my daughter get tossed into the air until she nearly touched the damn ceiling. I've seen her clothes magically rip off of her body. I've seen the bed shake, like if we were hit by the Big One. I've taken her to a doctor and I just don't believe his explanation. It's not a mental problem. There's something wrong here."

Reina sighed upon finishing her passionate explanation. She closed her eyes and lowered her head, waiting to be ridiculed. Rose didn't laugh, though. Although she couldn't remotely verify the authenticity of Reina's claims, she felt the mother's pain.

Rose said, "It would be our pleasure to investigate your home, Ms. Knight. There are several things we must make clear first, though."

"Like what?"

"Well, I need you to understand that, if we approve this investigation, you will be paying for our travel. Secondly, you'll have to fill out several consent forms as well as other legal documents. And, thirdly, you will have to give us proof of a haunting-slash-happening in your house before we even get started."

"Proof? What kind of proof do you need?"

"Unaltered photos or videos of the haunting. You said you've seen the bed shake. If you captured unaltered footage of that, that could convince us to visit you. The better the proof, the more likely I can convince my partner to approve a trip to your house.

Okay?"

Determination in her eyes, Reina said, "*Okay,* I'll get the proof you need."

Chapter Thirteen

Evidence

Reina slinked into Julie's bedroom, her cell phone in hand. She closed the door behind her and made sure to turn the lock. She didn't want Nick to interfere. She turned and looked around the room—confused, anxious, *frightened.* Three days had passed since the doctor's last house call. She had been in-and-out of the bedroom since then, taking care of Julie to the best of her ability, but she was still caught off guard by the room's malevolent aura.

The seemingly impenetrable darkness didn't help, either. All of the bulbs on the fairy lights were shattered. Moonlight seeped past the blinds on the windows across the room, but it wasn't enough to illuminate every dark corner. Fortunately, she opened an app and used the flash on her phone's camera as a light. The unusually dense darkness wasn't the only anomaly in the room, though.

Reina crossed her arms and rubbed her shoulders. Her bottom lip quivered and her shoulders trembled. She could see each exhale, clouds blooming from her mouth. Although the windows were closed, the room was colder than usual. The cold sensation felt inexplicably evil, too. A temperature never felt so ominous.

Reina illuminated the bed with her phone. She couldn't help but smile. Julie lay in bed, breathing throatily. She appeared to be sleeping—*finally.*

Reina flicked the light switch near the door. She

expected the lamps on the nightstands to turn on, but the room remained dark.

She whispered, "They're broken, too... How is this happening?"

She shook her head and proceeded with her plan. From her left, she took a picture of her daughter with the flash on. She moved towards the foot of the bed, then she took another photo. She ended up on the other side of the room where she took one final photo of Julie on the bed. She stopped the make-do photoshoot and took a moment to cycle through the photos.

She was saddened by the pictures. Julie's face was hollow—she hadn't had a decent meal in weeks. She had bruises on her cheeks, as if she were slapped by a powerful person. Her lips were dry, flaky, and pale. The bandages around her forearm were stained with dried blood. Her pajamas and bed sheets were soaked in urine.

Reina grimaced and whispered, "I'm sorry, baby. I'm getting help for us now. Just stay strong for a little longer..."

She walked around the bed and began photographing every corner of the room, glass crackling under her slippers with each step. She opened another app to keep her flash on at all times, then she started to record a video.

Befuddled, Reina narrowed her eyes and carefully recorded every corner of the room. As if she had walked into a room in an abandoned house, the bedroom appeared old and dilapidated. The walls were chipping and crumbling, stained with mold. The windows were cracked and smudged. Splinters protruded from the cracked floorboards. The malevolent presence in the home grew stronger.

Reina stopped as she reached the dresser near the door. She heard a *crackling* sound behind her. It was the sound of someone stepping on glass. Someone else was moving in the room. Her breathing intensified and her hands trembled. She thought: *is it going to attack me next?* She took a deep breath, then she turned around.

To her utter surprise, there was no one there. She slowly turned, gliding her light over every inch of the room, then she stopped upon reaching the bed. She practically juggled the phone as it slipped in her hands.

Julie was gone.

Reina staggered towards the foot of the bed. She said, "Julie, please come out. Show yourself, sweetheart. Don't... Don't do anything you'll regret. Please, baby, I'm only trying to help you."

There was no response. An eerie dead silence dominated the bedroom. She looked over at the windows to her right. She could see leaves dancing with a gust of wind, but she couldn't hear the *whooshing* or the *crackling*. It was as if the room were in a dimension of its own, whisked away from the earthly realm.

Before she could utter another word, Reina felt something moist on the back of her neck—like someone breathing heavily over her shoulder. She heard the peculiar breathing, too, raspy and irregular. The hairs at the back of her neck prickled with each breath, causing her to shudder uncontrollably. She closed her eyes and shook her head. *There's no one there, there's no one there*—she repeated the phrase in her head over and over, like a child hiding from the bogeyman under her bed sheets.

She hopped and yelped as she felt a soft touch under her ears. The gentle pressure moved across her cheeks, as if someone were caressing her face. At first, it felt like an insect—a spider or a roach—was skittering across her cheeks. It made her skin crawl. She eventually recognized the touch, though—*fingertips.* They were the softest fingers she ever felt. The tender touch made her feel uncomfortable, though. She didn't know who—*or what*—was touching her face after all.

Reina stumbled towards the bed, then she quickly turned around and illuminated the room. Julie stood behind her, grinning from ear-to-ear. Somehow, her daughter managed to sneak behind her without being noticed.

Reina held her phone in her right hand while holding her left hand up in a peaceful *gesture—wait, I come in peace.* She didn't stop recording, though. Although her daughter's mental health worried her, she was certain a supernatural force was at play. She needed evidence in order to save Julie.

Reina pleaded, "Julie, please stop this. I'm just trying to help you, sweetie. Please, let me help you."

In a hoarse tone, Julie responded, "Hello, *sweetie.* Did you come to have some 'fun' with me? I was getting bored in here by myself. I keep touching and touching, but I think I need another hand." She slowly slid her hand across her stomach until she reached her crotch. She smirked and said, "This body... we have it all to ourselves. You can kiss me... No, you can *lick* me wherever you please. We can have fun with the girl's body while she's gone. Don't you want to touch it? Hmm? Haven't you ever thought about

Her Suffering 125

touching your own daughter? Fingering her pussy? Flicking your tongue at her clit?"

Reina grimaced in disgust, appalled by the deviant suggestions. However, she didn't believe her daughter was responsible for the words. The confrontation supported her other outlandish theory: Julie was possessed.

Scowling, Reina said, "You're not Julie, you're not my baby girl."

"Oh, *really?* How long did it take you to figure that out, genius?"

"Who are you? What do you want with my daughter?"

Julie continued to smile, but she didn't respond.

Reina shouted, "Who are you?!"

Julie stomped and shrieked at the top of her lungs. The bloodcurdling screech caused the floor to shake, the furniture to tremble, and the windows to shatter. The phone slipped out of Reina's hands, landing between her slippers.

Terrified, Reina fell to her knees and grabbed the phone. She crawled away from the foot of the bed, scampering to the other side of the bedroom, then she turned towards the center of the room with her cell phone in hand. The astonishment on her face was clear—a raised brow, wide eyes, and quivering lips.

The room changed back to normal after she dropped her phone. The lights were still broken, but the walls were clean and solid. The windows remained intact, too. Julie lay on her bed, breathing noisily as she slept. It looked as if nothing had actually happened in the room.

Reina stopped the recording. She opened the door, then she stepped into the doorway. She took one final glance at the room, still in disbelief. She slinked out of the room and closed the door behind her. She looked over at Nick's door. To her relief, the boy didn't hear a thing.

As she walked back to the living room, Reina scrolled through the photos of the bedroom and watched the footage. She had to make sure it actually happened before she sent it to Unearthly Happenings. Part of her wanted to believe it was all a vision, her daughter could be cured with medicine and the supernatural did not exist, but the evidence depicted the opposite.

Julie was under attack by a supernatural entity—and that entity wanted the world to know about it.

Reina connected her phone to her laptop, she transferred the files, she emailed them to Rose, then she waited for her call. She sat in the living room for forty-five minutes, her eyes glued to the hallway. She thought about Julie, Nick, and her deceased husband, Richard. A bubbly ringtone emerged from her laptop's speakers—Rose was calling.

Reina quickly answered the call. She could read Rose like a children's book. The young woman was amazed by the evidence.

Reina asked, "Was it enough for you and your partner? Will you help my daughter?"

Rose grinned and said, "*Yes.* We will happily investigate your home, ma'am. It will be our honor."

Reina smiled and sighed in relief. She said, "Oh, God, thank you... Thank you so much."

"The pictures, the footage... What you've captured is truly amazing. We took a few minutes to look for any altercations, but we couldn't find any. This is... This is *impressive*, Ms. Knight. It is a spectacle of supernatural activity. It's something that we've never seen before. *But,* I still have to give you a serious warning. If this footage has been altered, you will *not* be given a refund. We'll also happily use your funds to take a little vacation if this is all some sort of publicity stunt. Okay?"

"I understand. I just want you to help my daughter."

"We will. We'll send you an invoice in a minute. We'll book a flight and we'll be out there by tomorrow night or the morning after. While we travel to you, I'd like you to send us a *detailed* email about your situation. Tell us *everything.* We want to prepare during the flight so we can begin as soon as we arrive."

Reina responded, "Okay, great. You have my email address. Send the invoice. I'll pay now and I'll send the email in an hour or two."

"Perfect. We'll talk to you soon, Ms. Knight."

The pair waved at each other, then the call ended. Reina's hope was rekindled during the call. She still felt an ominous presence in the house, evil lurked in the darkest corners, but she was relieved to know that her saviors were on the way. She wiped the tears from her eyes, then she began composing the email.

Chapter Fourteen

Unearthly Happenings

Knocking echoed through the home. Reina and Nick, washing and drying dishes at the sink, turned and looked over at the archway. They glanced at each other and smiled—*the cavalry has arrived.* The pair dropped the dishes in the sink and rushed to the front door, like children eager to meet their father after a hard day's work.

Reina wiped her hands on her robe, she took a deep breath to clear her mind, then she opened the door.

Rose Love and Edmund Kowalski stood on the front porch. Rose clasped her hands in front of her chest and smiled. Although the situation was bleak, the young woman refused to lose hope. Edmund, a middle-aged man with feathery brown hair, frowned as he struggled to carry three bags in his arms. He was the technical expert, but he was also treated as the lackey.

Reina stepped to the side and said, "Come in, come in. Do you need a hand?"

Edmund sighed, then he said, "It's fine, miss. Just tell me where I can set all of this down. There's more in the car, actually, so we need quite a bit of space."

"Oh, well, you can set it down anywhere in the living room and kitchen."

Rose clapped and said, "Great. While Edmund unpacks, you and I should talk about this... *situation,* if you will." She glanced back at Edmund and said,

"Unpack and start setting up the equipment, okay? We need cameras and microphones everywhere. *Everywhere*, Edmund."

"Everywhere," Edmund repeated. "I got it, I got it."

Reina furrowed her brow as she listened to their conversation. She knew about Unearthly Happenings, but she wasn't aware of the show's production process. She could only smile and nod as she led Rose to the living room.

As she sat on the sofa, Reina said, "Nick, go to your room."

Nick responded, "But, mom, I want to see them set–"

"Please, go to your room," Reina interrupted. Nick sighed in disappointment, then he trudged down the hall and went to his room. As Rose sat beside her, Reina said, "My son has seen some of the... the *things* that have happened to Julie, but I don't want him to get involved if he doesn't have to."

Rose responded, "That's fine. I won't force you to do anything you're not comfortable with." She reached into her bag and pulled out a contract—a stack of papers. She placed the stapled sheets of paper and a pen on the table in front of them, then she said, "This is the contract I was telling you about. I emailed you a copy two nights ago, so I hope you had time to read over it. I'd like to get down to business as soon as possible, but... well, we have to protect our interests."

Reina stared down at the thick stack of papers. Since the couple arrived a day later than expected, she spent the previous day reading over the contract. It included forms concerning liability and consent. She understood most of it and none of it seemed malicious. Still, she didn't know how her daughter would react on camera. She glanced over her shoulder as Edmund walked into the living room.

The man began unpacking the bags. He pulled out laptops, monitors, cameras, microphones, and other devices she couldn't identify. The man appeared to be struggling with dozens of tangled cords, too. The group had an armory of investigative equipment. Unearthly Happenings was a web-show, but Rose and Edmund were serious about the business.

One-by-one, Reina signed the sheets of paper.

As Reina signed the last sheet, Rose said, "Great. Now we can talk business. First of all, Edmund is going to set up cameras in the living room, the hallway, and Julie's bedroom. We won't record anything you don't want us to record, but we need to have our eyes open at all times. Would it be okay if we set up a... a makeshift surveillance headquarters here in the living room?"

Makeshift surveillance headquarters, Reina thought, *what the hell is she talking about?* She looked over at Edmund. The man stared back at her, obviously waiting for her response. Reina simply nodded—*yeah, sure.*

Rose said, "Good. So, your email was great. It was very helpful. I have a few questions, though."

"O–Okay. What do you need to know?"

"Has anything out of the ordinary or supernatural occurred in any of the other rooms in the house? I only ask because I'm not exactly feeling anything in this room. From my experience, when a home is haunted, I could feel it from the front gate. It's even possible for me to feel it a few minutes *before* I even arrive. It's different here, though. It's almost like it's...

it's being masked by something."

Reina understood Rose's doubt. She couldn't feel the ominous aura in the home, either. It was as if the wicked spirit tormenting Julie had retreated before the parapsychologists arrived.

Reina explained, "It, um... It mostly happens in Julie's room. I've actually never seen it anywhere else in the house. She won't come out of her room, either."

"I see. But you said she was attacked at a friend's house, right?"

"Yes. She was babysitting and then there was a... an accident. That was when things started to get more... *violent.* I didn't see it happen, but she said it was the same ghost or demon or *whatever* it is that attacked her."

Rose glanced over her shoulder, peering down the hall. She tilted her head, like a curious dog listening to peculiar sounds.

She said, "Interesting... If that's the case, I'd say it's not the house that's haunted, it's your daughter. An evil spirit may have latched onto her."

"Why?"

"We'll find out soon enough."

As he entered the living room, Edmund said, "After we set up our equipment, it'll be fairly simple for us to track whatever is tormenting your daughter, Ms. Knight. When Rose meets Julie for the first time, I'll set up cameras in her room. That's okay with you, correct?"

Reina said, "Yes, I've already signed the waivers."

"That's good, but do you understand the dangers of proceeding? Once I set up the equipment, we may not be able to turn back."

"Wha–What do you mean?"

"Start setting up the equipment in the living room, Edmund. I'll explain it to her," Rose said. She turned in her seat and gazed into Reina's eyes. While Edmund dealt with the equipment, Rose explained, "What Edmund means is: certain complications may arise during procedures like this. We'll be opening a lot of doors to places we don't fully understand. And, sometimes, things may not go the way we expect. People have died during situations like this. Now, no one has ever died under *our* watch, but it's always a possibility. Once we set those cameras up, once I start talking to her, we'll be opening a door we might not be able to close. You have to understand that."

Reina responded, "I understand it. I understand it completely. I don't know if... if you're the real deal, but I'm out of options. This is my last chance at keeping my daughter here—at saving her. I only want you to promise me one thing: if you don't think it's something supernatural and you believe it may be a mental illness, I want you to tell me the truth. I don't want to believe it's all in her head, but I'll send her to a hospital if I have to."

Rose nodded in agreement. She stared at Reina in wonderment. She was pleasantly surprised by her dedication to her daughter.

She said, "We're not going to capitalize off of this in any, um, extravagant way. If we're successful, Julie will appear on our show, but her identity will be protected. We won't make a show out of her if it's not a haunting, though. Oh, and before I forget: for our safety and hers, you need to understand that your daughter may be restrained if she becomes dangerous. Okay?"

"I understand. It might be for the better anyway. I

don't want her to hurt herself again."

"We won't let that happen," Rose responded, smiling. She glanced over at the hall and asked, "Is she in the second room to the right?"

"Yes."

"Okay. I think I should go talk to her. Edmund, are you ready?"

Edmund, tangled in cords and surrounded by bags, puckered his lips and shook his head. He knew Rose was eager to work, though. So, he grabbed a bag filled with wireless surveillance cameras and he lunged away from his mess.

He said, "Alright, Rose. I'm ready."

Rose smirked and said, "Good. Let's go meet Julie."

***

Rose entered the bedroom, Edmund followed closely behind. Rose was empty-handed while Edmund lugged a bag full of gadgets. The door was left cracked open in order to test the suspected entity's strength—*was it limited to Julie and the room or could it escape at will?*

As Edmund examined the room for the best places to install the cameras, Rose walked to the foot of the bed with her hands clasped behind her back. With a keen eye for ghostly details, she inspected Julie and the bed. Curiosity and suspicion influenced her decisions.

Julie lay in bed, delirious. She smiled and giggled as she watched her visitors. She welcomed them to her room with open arms. She wasn't baited by the open door, either. At heart, she knew she was never locked in the room. She could have walked out weeks ago. She wasn't interested in the outside world, though.

Rose whispered, "In the name of Jesus Christ and everything holy, we ask for protection from the evil spirits and entities in this house. We ask for peace, light, and righteousness during our darkest times. Amen."

"What was that?" Julie asked in a squeaky, childish voice.

Rose furrowed her brow and responded, "Excuse me?"

"*That.* What you just said."

"Oh. It's a small prayer for protection. It's nothing for you to be worried about."

"I'm not worried about it. It just sounded... *stupid.*"

One side of Rose's mouth rose in a half-smile. She was amused by Julie's playful insult. She walked closer to the foot of the bed, examining the urine-and-feces soaked bed sheets. She wasn't put off by the stench, though. She was young but experienced. She had seen and smelled worse during her career.

The medium asked, "How are you feeling, Julie?"

"I'm feeling fine—perfectly fine. Why do you ask?"

"Well, you look... *sick.* Battered. Bruised. Malnourished. You don't look 'perfectly fine' to me, Julie."

"You don't look fine to me, either."

Rose chuckled. Again, she was not nervous. She was simply amused. She looked back at Edmund. Although he focused on his equipment, Edmund constantly glanced back at the bed. He was the cameraman, the tech-guy, and the muscle.

Rose turned her attention to Julie and asked, "If you're 'perfectly fine,' if everything is fine and dandy, why haven't you gone to work recently?"

"Work? I don't work, silly. I'm just a child."

"A child? Like, a little girl?"

Julie smirked and nodded.

Rose said, "Oh, I see. In that case, why don't you play outside? Why don't you play with the other kids?"

"I like to play *inside.* I like to play with dolls—dolls that look like people. And, when I break my dolls, they *hurt* people in real life. So, even though I'm inside, it really is like I'm playing with other people *outside.* I like that."

"You like... hurting people?"

"Yup. It's fun. It's fun and it's funny. You wouldn't understand. You're too old to have fun like us kids."

Rose carefully analyzed Julie's behavior. From her squeaky voice to her juvenile demeanor, Julie appeared to be portraying herself as a child. Judging from her statements—playing with dolls that hurt people—she wasn't exactly innocent.

Rose asked, "I'm not talking to Julie, am I? Who are you?"

Julie giggled, then she said, "My name is Marie—*Marie Brooks.* Everyone knows me. I'm 'Sweet Marie,' you know?"

"May I speak to Julie?"

"No, ma'am. She's in time-out. She's not allowed to talk to anyone. Besides, it's my turn to talk."

My turn to talk—the words echoed through Rose's mind. The pieces to the puzzle were connecting, but she couldn't see the full picture. She narrowed her eyes and tilted her head. She felt something in the room. It wasn't Julie, it wasn't Marie. It was an ominous presence that gently stroked the back of her neck—*mocking her.*

Rose said, "There's someone else here, isn't

there?" As he installed a camera onto the computer desk, Edmund glanced back at the bed—*baffled.* Rose said, "Yes, there's a man. A strong man. May I speak to him? May I speak to the man who started it all?"

Shaking her head, Julie smiled and said, "I don't think so, ma'am. It's my turn and–"

She stopped speaking mid-sentence. The smile was wiped from her face, twisted into a grimace of pain. She tightly squeezed her eyes shut and squirmed on the bed. The muffled sound of bones *popping* emerged from her body. She whimpered and moaned, as if she were feeling immense pain. Veins bulging from her neck, she gasped and sat up in bed, then she fell back down to the mattress with a loud *thump.*

In a gruff voice, deep and masculine, Julie asked, "What do you want from me?"

Rose and Edmund looked at Julie with wide, protuberant eyes. They had experience with the supernatural, but they never witnessed such a drastic change during such a short amount of time. Julie looked the same, but her voice and demeanor were radically different.

Rose glanced over at Edmund and said, "Don't stop. Keep installing." Edmund sighed as he reluctantly proceeded. Rose looked back at Julie and asked, "Who are you?"

"Take a guess."

"No, I don't think I will. We're not playing games today. Who are you?"

"*Guess.*"

"No. I won't humor you. Do you even know who you are?"

Julie huffed, then she said, "Richard. I'm Richard."

"Richard?"

"*Richard Knight,* you stupid cunt."

Rose and Edmund were taken back by the hostile response. They remained calm and prepared, though.

Rose said, "Richard... You're, um, Julie's father. I have to ask: do you realize you're dead?"

"Of course I do. What do you think? Huh? You think I'm stupid? You think I'm brain-dead? Is that it?"

"No, I'm just confused. No, no, scratch that. I'm not 'confused,' that's the wrong word. I'm curious. What do you want with Julie?"

Julie cackled, then, speaking as Richard, she said, "This is my girl, *my pussy,* and I'm not leaving. Do you understand me?"

"Why? Why won't you leave? What do you want with her?"

Julie stared down at her body and sneered in disgust. She said, "This whore... She deserves to burn for what she did. You see, I didn't do anything wrong. When she was six, seven, eight... I don't really remember how old she was when it happened, but *she* seduced *me* when she was a child. She saw that I was drunk and she seduced me. I knew she would tell eventually, so I had to run... and then I crashed my damn bike and I died. It's fucked up. She should be dead and burning, *not me.*"

Rose could see Richard's spirit was restless. The malevolent spirit believed he was dealt a bad hand. He shifted the blame for his horrendous actions to his victim. Even in death, he mustered the audacity to blame his daughter for the molestation.

Julie barked, "Fuck you, too! If you think you're going to get rid of me, you're wrong! I'll kill her before you kill me again!"

Edmund tapped Rose's shoulder and said, "There has been an alarming surge of paranormal activity here, Rose. I know you feel it. We should get out. *Now.*"

Rose responded, "Wait a second, Ed. We're–"

Before she could utter another word, Rose yelped as she levitated from the ground—her feet dangling two feet above the floor. She felt a strong pressure on her stomach, as if she were being pushed. She could feel herself floating in reverse, soaring towards the desk behind her.

Edmund dropped his bag and dashed behind Rose. He grabbed her in mid-air. The pair crashed into the computer chair, causing it to roll away, then they fell to the floor in front of the desk.

As the couple recovered from the attack, Julie sat up in bed and said, "I'm going to kill everyone in this house—you, your lackey, the cheating whore, that stupid boy, and this disgusting cunt."

She crawled to the edge of the bed and reached for the nightstand. She unscrewed the broken light bulb from the lamp. Sharp shards of glass still protruded from the cap of the bulb. She hopped off the bed, then she scampered towards the couple—using her hands and feet to rush forward with a hunched back.

Edmund quickly staggered to his feet. He grabbed Julie's wrists and stopped her from attacking them. They grappled across the room until Edmund pushed her back onto the bed. He ran back to Rose's side and helped her stand. The pair, disoriented and horrified, glanced over at the bed as Julie shrieked.

Using Richard's deep voice, Julie shouted, "You can't take her! The whore is mine!"

She held the bulb up, then she stabbed down at her

crotch. The glass penetrated her groin, causing blood to squirt onto the bed sheets under her. She raised her arm, then she thrust downward again. The glass penetrated her vulva, mutilating her genitals. A shard even snapped off and remained jammed in her vulva as she pulled the bulb away from her crotch.

Edmund grabbed a set of handcuffs from his bag, then he ran to the bed. He stopped Julie from stabbing herself again, pushing her wrist down to the edge of the bed. Despite her resistance, he was able to handcuff her to the nearest bedpost.

He shouted, "Rose! Grab the handcuffs! Hurry!"

Rose snapped out of her fear-induced trance. She quickly gathered the other handcuffs. She tossed a pair at Edmund as she ran towards the bed. The pair cuffed Julie's other wrist and ankles to the bedposts. They regrouped at the foot of the bed, horrified.

They simultaneously gasped and trembled as a cluster of black widow spiders skittered out of her bloody vagina. The sound of their legs *crackling* with each step echoed through the room. The spiders crawled across her legs, her abdomen, and the bed. Dozens became hundreds in a matter of seconds.

As soon as they blinked, however, the spiders disappeared. The young woman's crotch was still bloody, but the spiders vanished into thin air. *Mind games,* Rose thought, *he's playing with us.*

As Julie hissed and snarled, angered by the restraints, Edmund said, "We have to leave."

Rose responded, "Yeah, yeah... Get your stuff. Come on."

The couple evacuated from the room. Edmund staggered down the hall while Rose closed the door behind her. The pair were clearly distraught, shocked by their first encounter with Julie. They couldn't keep a semblance of control, either.

From the end of the hall, Reina asked, "What happened?"

Rose and Edmund glanced over at Reina, speechless. They looked at each other, searching for a sense of direction—*what do we do now?*

Rose swallowed the lump of anxiety in her throat, then she said, "We might have a little problem. Edmund, go over to the closest hardware store. Buy some security bars and put them over Julie's windows." Edmund marched out of the house, rattled but determined. Rose turned towards Reina and said, "We have to talk, but... let's wait until Edmund comes back, okay? He's my... my pillar of support, if you will. Let's, um... Let's sit in the living room."

Reina didn't have any other options, so she agreed with her. As Rose approached, she wrapped her arm around her and helped her reach the sofa. She understood the shock of facing such a powerful supernatural force. She had experienced it for herself after all.

***

Hours had passed since the violent encounter in Julie's bedroom. After Julie fell asleep, Reina and Rose entered the room to treat the teenager's wounds. Meanwhile, Edmund spent the afternoon modifying the home, installing security bars outside of Julie's windows and latch locks on her door.

At dusk, Reina, Rose, and Edmund met over fresh coffee in the living room. With his bedroom door cracked open, Nick sat near the doorway and eavesdropped on the meeting.

Rose sighed, then she said, "So, I guess I should

explain what happened. I just don't know where to start."

"From the beginning," Reina said. "What happened in there? How did my daughter get those cuts? I mean, Christ, you *just* met her and she's already hurt. She... She's mutilated!"

"We didn't hurt her, Reina. We went in there and performed our preliminary investigation—for lack of a better term. While Ed was setting up the cameras, I interviewed Julie. At first, she was talking like a child. I don't have an explanation for that yet. However, after that, she began talking like her father... or who we could only assume was her father."

"Ri–Richard?"

"Yes. Richard claimed he was possessing your daughter's body. If that's true, then he is also responsible for the self-harm. She couldn't attack us, so she attacked herself with a broken light bulb."

"Oh, God... What's happening? Richard possessed Julie? He forced her to attack herself? Are you serious?"

Reina dug her fingers into her hair and leaned back in her seat, befuddled by the revelation. Rose rubbed her shoulder, trying her best to comfort her. Edmund typed away on his laptop, occasionally mumbling to himself.

Rose said, "I don't believe this is a normal haunting or possession. I think an incubus has attached itself to Julie."

Reina stuttered, "Wha–What's an incubus?"

"An incubus is a demon in male form who preys on women. In layman's terms, this demon's goal is to engage in sexual activity with a human female. The woman is usually sleeping before the attack, but it can attack at any moment. Some women even enter 'consensual' relationships with these demons, allowing them to rape them at will. Regardless of the victim's resistance, the incubus will rape her until her health deteriorates."

"Until she... dies?"

Rose frowned and nodded—*exactly.*

"Marie Brooks," Edmund interrupted. He turned towards Rose and said, "That theory might not be correct, Rose. At least not completely. I searched the name Julie gave us when she was speaking like a child. She said her name was Marie Brooks."

"So?" Rose responded, confusion laced into her voice.

"Marie Brooks was a serial killer from the 1930s. Although she wasn't officially diagnosed by doctors at the time, early sessions showed she may have suffered from dependent personality disorder or dissociative identity disorder. She lived her life believing she was a child. And... And she *supposedly* used voodoo dolls to kill her bullies. Unless Julie had a very deep interest in the macabre, I don't believe she would know all of this. I just... I don't think it's possible, Rose."

Rose responded, "I understand. Perhaps she is being attacked by more than one spirit, maybe she's attracting a *horde* of wicked entities. I think it could be possible, but... but I still think the incubus is the main problem here. And I believe that incubus is Richard Knight. If we get rid of Richard, we'll get rid of Marie and anyone else who may be hiding in Julie's body."

With a newfound sense of determination flowing through her, Reina said, "Okay, okay. So, how do we get rid of it?"

"Although I believe an exorcism may work, I have to ask a few experts just to be sure. For now, I think we should keep Julie in a controlled environment. We shouldn't do anything to antagonize her. We just need a little bit of time."

Reina, Rose, and Edmund stared down the hall—curious, anxious, *horrified.* Through the crack on his door, Nick stared at Julie's bedroom. The atmosphere in the home was tense and ominous, smothering the occupants like a pillow over a person's face. Everyone had questions, but no one had answers. They could only wait and see.

Chapter Fifteen

Deviant Lust

Drenched in a cold sweat, Julie coughed and turned as she lay on her bed. Her mother and the parapsychologists slept in the living room down the hall while her brother slumbered in his bedroom, but she couldn't sleep. The tormented teenager was trapped between consciousness and unconsciousness—between the nightmares of reality and the nightmares of sleep.

"Julie, Julie, Julie," a deep, masculine voice said from the corner of the room.

Writhing in discomfort, Julie glanced over at the corner. She could barely see the other person in the room—her vision was blurred and the room was dark—but she recognized the voice. Standing in the darkness, her father interrupted her attempt to sleep.

Julie grimaced and whispered, "What do you want from me?"

Richard chuckled, then he said, "I want you to suffer, girl. You don't deserve to live. Your life is worthless. Just look at yourself. You're pathetic. Give up. Kill yourself. *Die.*"

"N–No..."

"No? *No?* You're just going to stay in bed for the rest of your life, huh? I shouldn't have expected anything else, I guess. You're a lazy whore, just like your mother. Speaking of that cunt, if you won't kill yourself now, it'll be my pleasure to watch her life crumble 'cause of you. She'll die trying to save you, then you'll die. Can you really let that happen? Won't you take the easy way out?"

Teary-eyed, Julie responded, "I won't do it. I *can't* do it."

"Why? Do you need a reason? It won't be hard to find one. Let's see... You're a failure. Your boyfriend's a failure. Your brother doesn't know what to think of you. And, 'cause of your burden, your mother is now a *fucking* failure. She can't climb the ladder of success while you drag her down. You've already wasted all of the family's money on doctors and 'ghost hunters.' You've ruined everything. Face it: you'd be better off dead."

Julie couldn't help but whimper. She felt like she was going crazy. Her father—a man who had been deceased for a decade—was trying to convince her to commit suicide. And, the man made sense. Depression tugged on her ankles and dragged her into an abyss of despair. She wasn't ready to quit, though.

She cried, "No, no, no. Just leave me alone."

Richard took a step forward. He said, "You're a little tougher than I imagined. I thought cutting up that filthy cunt of yours would have done the trick. I hate to admit it, but... I was wrong. You can't give up, can you? You're just too attached to this bullshit world, aren't you?"

Scowling, Julie responded, "Just like you, you sick bastard. That's why you're still here, that's why you won't leave."

Richard smirked and said, "Like father, like daughter." He took another step forward, but Julie still couldn't see him clearly. He asked, "What are you attached to, girl? We both know you have nothing to live for, so why won't you kill yourself? Do you actually like it here? Do you enjoy sinning?"

"No."

"Can't give up on your boyfriend's dick, can you? Or... Or is it your little brother? Hmm?"

"Wha–What?"

Julie blinked erratically as she tried to clear her vision. Before her very eyes, Richard shrunk and transformed into Nick. The boy—wearing his baby blue pajamas—grinned as he approached the bed.

In his soft, tender voice, he said, "Hey, Julie. I'm sorry I haven't been able to see you so much lately. Mom's keeping your room on lock-down, you know?"

Tears streaming down her cheeks, Julie stuttered, "It–It's okay."

"It's not okay. I really want to help 'cause... 'cause I love you. It's scary, though. When you change, I just don't know if you love me, too. Do... Do you love me?"

Julie sniffled and snorted, but she couldn't swipe at the mucus dripping from her nose. She struggled to comprehend the situation, but she was relieved to hear her brother's voice. The boy brought a sense of normality to her life. At that moment, the foreboding aura was whisked away and she finally felt safe.

She said, "Of course I love you, kiddo."

"So, would you do anything for me?"

"Of course. I'd give my life for you."

In a distorted voice, slow and sonorous, Nick responded, "Really? That's good. That's great. I've been watching you, Julie. I watch you while you sleep, while you shower, while you masturbate... Can you help me masturbate, too? Then, maybe I can help you. A favor for a favor? It's fair, isn't it? You love me, don't you?"

Julie grimaced in disgust. She was shocked by his sudden change and appalled by his vulgar request. At heart, she knew it wasn't really her brother, but it still *felt* like it was him.

As he approached the bed, Nick said, "I know you've thought about it before. You've thought about touching me, haven't you?"

"No. No, *never*. Please go away... Please..."

Nick giggled deliriously. The laughter was raspy, loud, and slow. He slid his thumbs under the waistband of his pajama pants, then he pulled his pants down. With his pants around his ankles, he waddled to Julie's side—shamelessly nude.

Julie cried, "No, damn it! No!"

Through her teary eyes, she couldn't see her brother's genitalia. She didn't *want* to see his privates anyway. Yet, she was drawn to him. She could not turn away from him, she couldn't give him the cold shoulder. The feeling resembled the same sensation she felt at Dr. Morris' office—she had entered an altered state. She was hypnotized by Richard, forced to continue the cycle of abuse.

As Nick stopped near her, Julie squirmed an inch away from the edge of the bed. She whimpered and shook her head, struggling to find a way out of the bizarre situation.

She said, "Stop. Don't do this."

Nick whispered, "Please, touch me like daddy touched you."

"No."

"Come on, you know you want to."

"No, I don't..."

"Pretty please? Can you–"

"I said stop!"

Her scream echoed through the house. Reina gasped as she awoke on the sofa, Rose quickly staggered off the recliner, and Edmund flopped on the floor as he struggled to escape from his blanket. The group sprinted down the hall, rushing to Julie's room.

Reina moved the bar latch that was installed onto Julie's door so she wouldn't escape, then she barged into the room. Rose and Edmund followed closely behind. From the doorway, they didn't see anything out of the ordinary in the bedroom.

Reina ran to the bed and asked, "What's wrong, baby? Are you there? Huh? Julie, is that you?"

Puffy-eyed, Julie stuttered, "Y–Yes... It's in the room. I'm scared, mom. I'm so scared. Hel–Help me..."

Reina glanced around, but she didn't see anything. She asked, "Where is it?"

"The corner near the desk..."

Reina and Rose pulled their cell phones out and illuminated the corners of the room with the flash of their cameras. Yet again, they didn't see anything out of the ordinary. Every corner of the room looked normal—exactly as they left it before they went to bed.

Before they could say a word, the lights on their phones darkened until the room was completely swallowed by the shadows. The darkness was not normal, though. It was thick, it was powerful, it was *impenetrable.*

Reina and the parapsychologists were blinded by the darkness. Their eyes had already adjusted to the dark after they awoke, but they couldn't see a thing in the room.

While the adults mumbled and staggered, Julie

looked over at the door and said, "Nick, come here."

Nick—the *real* Nick—already stood in the doorway to her room, peering inside with inquisitive eyes. He glanced over at the adults and furrowed his brow. He could see in the dark and he could hear Julie's voice, but the adults appeared to be blind and deaf.

Weak, Julie said, "Please, come here."

Nick reluctantly entered the room. Floorboards creaking under his bare feet, he quietly crept towards the bed.

While the adults stumbled about, Julie said, "Nick, I... I had a vision. I have a bad feeling in my stomach. You know, like the feelings mom gets when she knows we're doing something we shouldn't be doing? That kind of feeling..."

Nick nodded. He knew all about Reina's motherly intuition.

Julie continued, "I'm afraid I'm going to hurt you and mom and everyone in this house. I really think I might hurt you, Nick. I might... I might abuse you."

"Why?"

"I think I'm... possessed. Whatever is inside of me, I think it wants me to hurt you. If things get out of hand, I want you to go to mom's room and get her gun. Then... Then, I want you to shoot me."

Nick's eyes widened upon hearing the request. He understood his sister's pain, he could feel it whenever she cried, but he couldn't understand her willingness to die. His bottom lip quivered as he cried.

He said, "I can't."

"You have to, Nick. I don't want to hurt you. Please, promise me. You'd be helping me, too. You'd end my pain. Promise me, Nick. Promise you won't let me hurt you or anyone else."

As he gazed into his sister's bloodshot eyes, Nick reluctantly nodded—*okay.* He swiped at his nose and rubbed his eyes, trying to remain strong for his sister. He couldn't imagine himself shooting his own sibling, but he was willing to do anything for her. He felt like he was supposed to fill his father's shoes, so he believed he had to protect his family by any means necessary.

Julie swayed her head and looked at the door, motioning her demands—*get out of here.* She said, "Go back to your room and go to sleep. I have to sleep, too. Go..."

Nick shambled out of the room, dejected by the encounter. From the doorway, he took one final glance back at Julie, then he walked back to his room. Julie watched her brother until the door closed behind him. She turned and stared at the ceiling. She violently shook on the bed, as if she were having a seizure.

Reina gasped and blinked rapidly. She could finally see in the dark. Rose and Edmund also regained their vision. Upon hearing the squeaky mattress, the adults glanced back at the bed. They watched as Julie convulsed on the mattress. Their eyes widened as the handcuffs miraculously snapped on their own.

Freed from the restraints, Julie slithered towards the headboard. She twitched and groaned, then she crawled *onto* the wall behind her bed. Bones popping with each sudden jerk, she crawled across the vertical wall until she reached the ceiling with her fingertips. She rubbed her torso and moist face on the wall as she moaned.

Reina, Rose, and Edmund watched in horror as she defied the laws of nature and broke the rules of gravity.

Upon reaching the ceiling, Julie shrieked at the top of her lungs. The sudden shriek caused Reina and Rose to fall to their knees. Edmund, on the other hand, teetered left-and-right as he struggled to keep his balance. They were overwhelmed by the shrill noise.

Like a spider hit with a shoe, Julie was flattened against the wall. Her body stiffened, her bones *crunched* and *popped,* then she fell from the wall and landed on the bed. A dead silence followed the incident.

Reina and the parapsychologists stared at the bed, dumbfounded. Julie rested in bed, handcuffed to the bedposts as if nothing had happened. She twitched and groaned, restless, but she was asleep. Mystified by the events, the adults quietly walked out of the bedroom. They regrouped in the hall and mumbled about the bizarre situation.

Chapter Sixteen

Surrender or Call for Backup

With midnight's arrival—only minutes after the event in Julie's bedroom—Reina, Rose, and Edmund gathered in the living room. The group sat on the same three-seat sofa as they remotely monitored Julie through a set of laptops connected to the cameras in her bedroom.

Reina held her robe up to her mouth, sniveling and trembling. Rose rubbed Reina's shoulder, trying to offer a sense of comfort and security. Edmund kept his eyes glued to the screen, analyzing every twitch on Julie's body.

Breaking the silence, Rose said, "We have to talk about what happened in there."

"About what happened in there?" Reina repeated in an uncertain tone, as if she were asking a question. "I don't think any of us can even begin to comprehend what the hell happened in there. It was like... like a scene from a damn horror movie, Rose. I thought you were going to help us stop this. That's why I paid you to come here. Why is it still happening? Why are we sitting around here *watching* her instead of *helping* her?"

Rose sighed, then she said, "I understand your frustration, Ms. Knight. Maybe I was a little insensitive. We don't have to talk about what happened in there. We all saw it. We should talk about what we're going to do next, though."

"And what's that? Hmm? What are you going to

do?! My daughter is dying in there for Christ's sake! What... What are we..."

Reina's unadulterated rage stopped her from forming a simple sentence. She began to slur her words as she wept. She felt guilty and weak, scared and confused. Mothers were supposed to protect their children—that was what she always believed. She couldn't protect Julie when she was a child and she couldn't protect her as an adult, and those facts devastated her.

Rose stroked Reina's hair and said, "It's okay. Everything's going to be okay. You have to be strong, alright? You don't want your daughter to think you've given up on her, right? You don't want your son to hear you crying, right?"

Although she was afraid, Reina agreed with the parapsychologist. *She's right,* she thought, *crying has never helped anyone.*

Yet, sitting next to his door, Nick still heard his mother's rants and cries. He buried his face in his knees and whimpered. He wanted to tell his mother about Julie's ominous message and request, but he couldn't muster the courage to speak up. Instead, he stayed in his room and cried as he eavesdropped on their conversation.

While Reina recomposed herself, Rose said, "I'm sorry we haven't been much help. Believe me, we're trying our best. This is just... This is something we've never truly experienced before. We've dealt with restless spirits, we've cleansed houses, but Richard is a completely different monster."

Reina sniffled and muttered, "Yeah, you're telling me..."

Rose said, "I am convinced—*one-hundred percent*

convinced—that Julie has been possessed by a 'demon.' I use the word 'demon' loosely here, though. It could be a demon, like something you'd hear about in the bible or like the ones you'd see in a movie, but I think it's an incubus or ghost. It's an entity."

"Whatever it is: *it's evil,*" Edmund said, never taking his eyes off of the screen.

Rose said, "Yes. It's the most wicked entity we've ever encountered. Aside from a few moments where she's conscious, Julie seems to have lost complete control of herself. To be blunt with you, Ms. Knight, if she's not saved soon, she *will* die."

Stony-faced, Reina clenched her jaw and glared at Rose. She was shaken by the disturbing revelation. Her heart shattered as regrets flooded her mind—*should I have taken her to a hospital? Will she die because of me?* Her bottom lip quivered as she grimaced. She cried, but she tried to keep the noise down. *Daughters bury mothers,* she thought, *I can't bury my little girl.*

In tears, she asked, "What do I have to do to save her? Do I... Do I call an ambulance? Huh? Do I have her committed?"

Rose responded, "I'm not sure that would make a difference. You saw it yourself. She was crawling on the walls. Or... she's able to manipulate what we're seeing so we *think* she's crawling on walls. Either way, she's doing the impossible."

"No. I don't know what I saw in there. Maybe we were wrong. Maybe *I* was wrong...."

Rose sighed and lowered her head. She understood Reina's frustration and confusion. She reached forward and grabbed her hand. She looked over at Edmund and Edmund glanced back at her. The couple communicated without uttering a sound. Edmund nodded—*go ahead, tell her.* Rose returned the nod—*okay.* She rubbed Reina's hand and took a deep breath.

Rose said, "Listen, Ms. Knight. I think there's still hope for your daughter. I think we can help her. We don't have to go to a hospital, either. There's another professional out there—someone with more experience than Edmund and I combined."

Reina stuttered, "R–Really? Wh–Who?"

"His name is Kisho Sato. Kisho doesn't have a web-show. He doesn't sell books, he doesn't perform 'rituals' on television. He's not known by mainstream audiences, but he is known around certain groups as a man with the ability to cast out demons."

Chiming-in, Edmund said, "He doesn't use equipment like us, but he's a professional. Like Rose, he's *very* spiritual. This man... He's not like other men. If anyone can get to your daughter at this state, if anyone can save her, it's him."

Reina leaned back in her seat as she digested the information. The parapsychologists painted an ideal situation: a hero would arrive at the house and rescue her daughter from the demons within. It all sounded too good to be true, though.

She asked, "What's the catch?"

Rose responded, "Well, things in this world aren't free. Kisho doesn't charge to exorcise demons. He will, however, need someone to pay for him to fly to the United States from Japan and he'll need someone to pay for his accommodation. That may cost well over a grand..."

Reina stared at Rose with a deadpan expression, then she looked at Edmund. She couldn't tell if they were legitimate parapsychologists or a pair of con artists—*friends or foes?*

She asked, "Are you kidding me? Is this some sort of elaborate scam? Huh? Now you need me to pay you so you can bring your friend over from Japan? Is that it? What? Are you all going to have a sleepover in *my* house while *my* daughter suffers?"

Edmund responded, "We're not scam artists, ma'am. This is just how the world works. Besides, we're in the process of making one of the greatest paranormal discoveries in history. This will change everything."

"My daughter is not a 'discovery,' Ed," Reina snapped. "She's not some ancient artifact in a museum or some tool to get more views for your damn show. She's a human being! She's my daughter!"

"I'm sorry, ma'am. That came out wrong. I–"

"Stop. Just stop it, okay?"

The living room became silent. Reina stared at her daughter on the monitor—confused, scared, *heartbroken.* Edmund frowned and shook his head, disappointed in himself. Rose continued to rub Reina's hand, the side of her mouth twitching with anxiety. She knew she couldn't save Julie by herself, but she had trouble admitting it.

The crimson-haired medium said, "Reina, this is your best option. I know we haven't made much progress, I know we haven't... *proven* ourselves to you. I know that very well and I'm sorry. It may feel like we're trying to scam you, but, I'm giving you my word: this *will* work. We'll even cover half of the cost to get Kisho to us."

Wide-eyed, Edmund asked, "We will?"

"Yes. We're about to make one of the greatest discoveries in paranormal history, aren't we?"

Edmund bit his bottom lip and shrugged. He wasn't fond of spending money, but he was willing to allow it—for Julie's sake. He bit his tongue and leaned back in his seat, allowing Rose to continue.

Rose said, "We either surrender now and see if medicine can explain how a woman can crawl on walls... or we call for backup. The choice is yours."

Reina gazed into Rose's glimmering eyes. She could see the young woman was sincere. The medium was willing to give up her payday in order to help Julie. Reina strongly considered calling Morris and sending Julie to a hospital. She was convinced the situation was of the supernatural kind, though—and a supernatural problem required a supernatural solution.

Reina said, "Okay. I have to... to organize my finances, but I'll do it. If this man can save my daughter, I'll give him everything I have in this world."

Rose said, "We'll do our best. I'll call him now. I don't think it's nighttime in Japan yet. I'll inform him about the situation on your behalf and I'll try to get him out here as soon as possible. It may take a few days, so we'll have to take care of Julie on our own until then."

"You–You're staying here, right?"

Rose smiled and said, "We're staying. The next few days will be rough, but we'll be by your side every step of the way."

Chapter Seventeen

The Arrival of Kisho Sato

"Get your hands off me, you dirty whore!" Julie shouted in a hoarse tone. She lunged forward and chomped at her mother, but the handcuffs pulled her back down to the mattress. She said, "I'm going to kill you, you filthy cunt. I should have done it a long time ago. You hear me? Yeah, I should have killed you in your sleep. I thought about suffocating you with a pillow so many damn times, but that would have been too easy—too *fucking* easy. Now, I'm going to make it hurt. I'm going to make you feel *real* pain, *real* suffering."

Reina cried as she staggered back, shocked by the threat of violence. She held a tray with a bowl of hot soup. The bowl and the spoon slid across the tray with each teetering step. She was only trying to feed her daughter. She didn't expect a verbal assault.

Rose rushed to Reina's side. She lifted the bowl from the tray, ensuring it didn't spill and burn Reina. Edmund stood at the foot of the bed, recording the event with a camcorder. Although he wanted to help, he was instructed to record everything—like the cameraman in a generic found footage horror movie.

The doorbell rang. Yet, Reina couldn't move. Stiff like a tree trunk, she stared at her daughter with a set of glum eyes. She was shocked by Julie's deteriorating condition—coarse, graying skin, sunken eyes, and hollow cheeks.

Julie was a petite woman before the first attack,

but she lost even more weight during the battle for her life. Her bones could be seen through her skin. Despite treatment, the cuts on her arms worsened. They looked yellow, crusty, and infected. She even developed a cut on her cheek and one on her thigh, but no one was around to see how they materialized.

Reina thought: *how did I let it get this far? Could the doctors have stopped this? Is this all my fault?* She couldn't shrug off the guilt and regret sitting on her shoulders.

From down the hall, Nick shouted, "Mom! Someone's at the door! Mom!"

Reina slowly shook her head as she snapped out of her trance. In disbelief, she glanced at Julie, then at Rose. She looked lost, as if she had just awoken from a dream and found herself in a nightmare. Rose placed the bowl on the tray, then she took the tray from Reina.

Rose said, "Answer the door. We'll take care of Julie. *Go.*"

Reina stepped into the hall, reluctantly closing the door behind her. She glanced over at Nick's room, and Nick stared back at her from his bedroom doorway. She could see the fear and curiosity in his eyes.

She said, "Stay in your room, Nick. Everything's okay."

Nick sighed and frowned as he closed his door. He still couldn't tell his mother about Julie's message. He was scared of telling the truth. Although he was never attacked or possessed, he felt as if he were being watched from the darkest corners of his room. If he interfered, he feared he would be attacked by the restless spirits that tormented his sister.

Reina walked to the front door. She kept her hand

on the wall every step of the way. She felt lightheaded, so she was afraid she would collapse before reaching her destination. She wiped the tears from her eyes and sniffled as she reached the door. She took a deep breath, then another one, then she opened the door.

Kisho Sato, a middle-aged Japanese man, stood on the porch. Long enough to cover his ears and brow, his black hair was silky and straight. He had a wispy mustache and a matching goatee. He wore a black coat over a black button-up shirt, black trousers, and matching dress shoes. He held a carry-on bag in his right hand. The man appeared benign—an angel on earth.

Reina was caught off guard by Kisho's appearance. She wasn't exactly attracted to him, despite his charming demeanor, but she inexplicably felt safe around him.

Reina said, "Konnichiwa."

Kisho chuckled, then he asked, "You speak Japanese?"

Surprised, Reina cocked her head back and asked, "You speak English?" She shook her head and blushed, embarrassed. She said, "I'm sorry. I was actually a little worried. My Japanese is a little rusty. You must be Kisho, right? If not, this little conversation might have just been a huge waste of time."

"I am Kisho—Kisho Sato. I am here to help in any way possible."

"Thank you. Thank you so much. Please, come in."

Kisho smiled and bowed, kind and respectful. He glanced around the home as he followed Reina to the living room. He examined the picture frames clinging to the walls and the equipment scattered across the floor. He wasn't bothered by the mess, though. He was a simple man with a complex past. He didn't expect the red-carpet treatment.

As they reached the living room, Rose and Edmund emerged from Julie's room. Edmund stopped recording upon spotting Kisho. Capitalizing off of hauntings was frowned upon in the community—but everyone had to work. Rose cracked a smile as she walked down the hall. Her dress and chest were drenched in soup.

Rose said, "Mr. Sato, it's good to see you. We've had quite a bit of trouble trying to cleanse this house."

Kisho responded, "I can see that. And, please, call me Kisho. Formalities aren't necessary during times like these."

A monstrous roar echoed from Julie's bedroom—*a battle cry.* The glass on the picture frames cracked with the roar. The frames even swung left and right on the walls.

Kisho asked, "How is she doing?"

"Well, I believe this is a case of possession. And, in terms of contact, I think we've lost her. She's still alive, but she's no longer responding. We should–"

"*Medically*, Rose," Kisho interrupted. "How is her breathing? How is her heart? How is her mind?"

"I can't answer everything for you. She's a fighter, so her heart is strong. She's a thinker, so her mind is still intact. She's battered, bruised, and cut, but she's still kicking. She might not be winning, but she's still fighting in there."

"Good, good."

Edmund asked, "Would you like to know more about the case?"

Kisho set his bag aside, then he said, "No, that

won't be necessary. I believe I know enough. Besides, I feel it would be best for all of us if I went in with a clear mind. Even with all of the information available at our fingertips, we never truly know the demons we will confront when we tangle with the great beyond." He glanced at Reina and smiled. He said, "I'll see what I can do. May I meet Julie alone? Without the cameras?"

Reina looked over at the parapsychologists. It wasn't her show, so she had to seek permission. She signed several contracts after all.

Rose said, "It's fine with us."

Edmund asked, "Are you sure about that? The cameras never interfered with any–"

"It's fine," Rose interrupted. She glanced back at Edmund and said, "Go disconnect them. Kisho needs his privacy."

Edmund sighed, but he didn't argue. They went to their laptops and disconnected from their network of remote surveillance. Reina gazed into Kisho's gentle eyes, communicating without uttering a word—*thank you for coming.* She patted his hand, then she joined the parapsychologists in the living room.

Kisho walked down the hall, ready to meet Julie.

***

Kisho entered Julie's bedroom and quietly closed the door behind him. He examined Julie's condition. She wasn't close to death, but she was clearly injured. The handcuffs on her wrists and ankles also bothered him. He wasn't afraid of her, though. As a matter of fact, he felt pity instead of fear. The young woman resembled a tortured prisoner in a serial killer's dungeon.

In a hoarse tone, Julie asked, "What are you

looking at, faggot? You're a few men short for a bukkake, aren't you?" As Kisho walked to the foot of the bed, Julie lunged forward and chomped at the air, snarling and growling like a feral dog. She said, "Do it. Touch me. Fuck me. Do something."

Kisho asked, "What is your name?"

"My name is Ted fucking Hall. The boys, the young ones, they call me 'Teddy.' Oh, yeah, they love playing with their *big* teddy bear. I love playing with them, too."

"Ted Hall... Well, Ted, may I speak to Julie? Is she available?"

"She's here somewhere, sure. You can't talk to her, though. Richard, that hard-ass, he won't allow it. *We* won't allow it. So, if you're not here to fuck me, why don't you fuck off?"

Kisho smiled—half-a-smile. He was disappointed by the response, but he wasn't dissuaded. They were having a conversation. Dialogue ultimately led to action and he was well aware of that. He lifted the computer chair from the floor and took a seat near the foot of the bed.

He said, "Ted, I don't want to hurt you. You aren't my enemy, you aren't my target. I only want to help Julie. Before I proceed with my plans, I need to know if she's okay. Do you understand?"

Julie cackled, then she said, "You're a nice, charming man. I wish I was as charming as you. I can only imagine the boys I could lure with your looks and charisma. Oh, I would love to be a suave gentleman. Just like you, Kisho, just like you..."

Despite hearing his name without properly introducing himself, Kisho wasn't disturbed by the entity's knowledge. He was a known exorcist in the human world, so he expected to be known in the supernatural realm.

He asked, "May I communicate with Julie?"

"No. But, because I like you so much, I'll cooperate a little. I know about Julie and Richard. Go ahead. Ask me anything."

"Very well. Is Julie alive in there?"

"Alive? Sure, sure. She's alive... but I can't promise she'll stay that way for long."

"Do you plan on killing her? Is that your goal?"

"My goal? No, I just like her body. I would have preferred something a little younger, but if it gets me closer to Nick, who am I to complain? Richard wants her to rot in hell, like him. It doesn't have to end in death, though. No, he might want to impregnate the cunt with his child so he can bring horror back to the world—so he can bring himself back. Then, maybe he'll kill her."

Although he was confused, Kisho kept a steady expression on his face. He didn't want to give the entity an advantage. The response was perplexing, though. He thought: *is Richard trying to reincarnate himself?* He had never heard of an incubus impregnating a human in order to come back to the human world.

Kisho asked, "Is Julie religious?"

"Is that a trick question? Are you trying to find out if I'm actually Julie? Hmm? Do you think this is fake?"

"No, no. Not at all. I'm simply looking for information."

"Oh, I see. Kisho, an exorcism won't work. Don't bother trying."

Kisho smirked and responded, "I could perform an exorcism. I have the experience and the power. It wouldn't be like the movies or even the documentaries. It would be unlike anything you ever experienced, Mr. Hall. I don't believe it's necessary, though."

"Good. Take the power of Christ and shove it up your ass."

Kisho gently chuckled and shook his head, amused by the vulgar response. He stood and walked to Julie's right.

He asked, "May I take a look?"

"Wha–What? What the hell are you talking about?"

Kisho reached forward and caressed Julie's moist brow. Eyes wide with fear, Julie squirmed away from the man's hand.

In her gruff voice, Julie asked, "What are you doing?"

Kisho said, "I am no longer talking to Ted Hall. I am talking to Julie Knight. Julie, can you hear me?"

Julie grimaced in pain. She grunted and groaned as she frantically shook her head. Her body jerked and trembled, the handcuffs *clinking* against the bedposts. Veins bulging from her brow and neck, she lifted her head from the pillow and gasped. Her eyes rolled back until only her yellow sclerae showed. Wheezing, she closed her eyes and fell back onto the bed.

Although her body was still bruised and sliced, Kisho could see Julie had changed. For the first time in days, she had control of her body.

Kisho said, "Julie, it's good to see you. We don't have much time. You must trust me. I am going to help you, but I need your permission. If you trust me, say 'yes.' If not, say 'no.' The choice is yours."

Julie's eyes flickered open and she found herself

staring at Kisho. She didn't have control of her body over the past week, but she could see and hear everything in her bedroom. It was as if she had retreated to the back of her mind and allowed a different personality to control her body. She didn't recognize Kisho, but she trusted him. There was something about his eyes that made her feel safe.

Teary-eyed, Julie stuttered, "Y–Yes."

Kisho smiled and said, "Thank you. Close your eyes, Julie. I'm going to take a look at the monster."

A tear streamed down Julie's cheek as she closed her eyes. Kisho pulled a necklace with a round silver pendant from out of his collar. A gate—which resembled a Torii Gate but not quite the same—was engraved on the pendant. He sat on the edge of the bed, disregarding any potential threats to his safety. He closed his eyes and placed the pendant on Julie's forehead.

***

Kisho opened his eyes. He was no longer in the teenager's bedroom. He miraculously awoke in a dark world—*Julie's mind.* He was surrounded by different shades of darkness, which distorted his vision. It was like taking a hallucinogenic drug and watching the walls melt, except there was no solid matter in sight. It appeared as if black fumes were emanating from the ground, billowing up to the dark sky.

Kisho pulled the necklace out of his collar, then he kissed the pendant. He walked forward with his head high, marching into the abyss. He had been there before and he wasn't afraid to delve deeper.

Voices emerged from the darkness, surrounding the spiritual man from every corner. The voices overlapped each other, so their words were incomprehensible. Some of the voices were loud and raspy, others were soft and feminine. The words couldn't be made out, but the languages were distinct—English, Spanish, Russian, and even Japanese.

Again, Kisho was not intimidated. With each step forward, his destination grew louder. He headed towards a large wrought-iron gate. Due to the dark color of the gate and the black sky, the top of the gate couldn't be seen from the ground—it was tall. However, the wide entrance was visible from afar. A dim white light glowed near the doors, calling to the wandering spirits in Julie's mind.

As he approached the gate, Kisho whispered, "There's more than I imagined..."

Scaly humanoid demons crawled on the gate, scampering like lizards. The demons were fast so they were difficult to see. Their wavering tails and flapping wings were visible, though. Humanoid silhouettes stood on the other side of the gate, lined up across the barrier as if waiting to purchase tickets to a popular concert. The shadowy figures, however, were only waiting to torment Julie.

Kisho stopped at the entrance. He didn't have to step through the opening. The spirit he sought—*Richard Knight*—stood at the gateway.

Richard had hardly changed since he first revealed himself at the diner. His hair was still curly, his stubble was still prickly. His eyes were completely blackened, though. He didn't wear any clothes, either, parading his nude body for the world to see—the *under*world. He appeared to be acting as the gatekeeper to Julie's mind and body. He allowed the spirits of Ted Hall and Marie Brooks—among others—to control Julie's body.

Julie was nowhere in sight. She was hiding somewhere in the dark world, still trying to fight for survival.

Kisho said, "You must be the one who wants to impregnate the girl... Richard Knight, correct?"

Richard smirked and responded, "Correct. And you must be the poor bastard my wife hired to fix her little problem, right? How much did she pay you? Or did she milk your dick for a favor just like she does for everyone else?"

"I wasn't compensated for this. At least, I won't be making any profit from this. I don't believe in capitalizing on pain and tragedy. I am here to help, though."

Richard stared at Kisho with a deadpan expression, then he burst into a chuckle. His laughter echoed through the dark world. Veiled by the darkness, the other demons and silhouettes snickered, too. The laughter was devious, eerie and wicked.

Kisho said, "You will not accomplish your goals, Richard. With all of these other demons around, Julie will most likely die before you'll be able to impregnate her—*if* that's even possible. And, even if you did impregnate her, she would certainly die before she would have the opportunity to give birth. This... This is all worthless. You understand that, don't you?"

"It doesn't matter to me. If I can't ruin her life, if I can't give that little whore a permanent reminder of me, then I'll happily watch her die. I'd stick around, too, just to watch her whore of a mother and her son suffer. Goals... I haven't had real goals in decades. The world killed my dreams, the world crushed my hope, so I'm going to burn it. Hell, even when this family is dead and gone, I'll stick around and start killing others. I might even start with you and those other fools Reina hired."

Kisho lowered his head and glanced to his right, then to his left. Although he couldn't see them, he could *feel* the horde of evil entities surrounding him. The demons were approaching from every angle, ready to pounce on Richard's demand.

Kisho said, "I understand. We'll meet again soon, Richard."

"I'm looking forward to it, *Kisho.*"

Kisho grabbed his necklace as he gazed into Richard's eyes. He felt like he was staring into the deepest crevice at the bottom of the ocean—*pure darkness.* He was looking into the eyes of true evil. He had spent decades exorcising demons, but Richard was a different type of entity. He broke the rules, so he was difficult to challenge.

As the demons approached, he closed his eyes and placed the pendant on his forehead. He felt his brain throbbing and heart pounding. The sensation made him feel like his skull would crack and his ribs would explode at any moment. He felt an inexplicable warmth across his body, as if lava were flowing through his veins.

Kisho opened his eyes. He was back in Julie's room, sitting beside the teenager on the bed. The room was unusually calm. As a matter of fact, the entire house was tranquil. He pulled the pendant away from Julie's moist forehead and tucked the necklace into his collar. He caressed her brow, pushing the hairs away from her forehead.

He whispered, "Stay strong, darling, stay strong..."

Julie's eyes swung open, wide and zany. With a raspy voice, she said, "We'll stay strong for you. We'll be waiting for you, Kisho."

Kisho sighed in disappointment. He was not defeated, though. Without saying another word, he departed from the room.

Chapter Eighteen

Options

Kisho sat in the recliner, one leg crossed over the other. Edmund paced back-and-forth on the other side of the coffee table, lost in his thoughts. Rose sat on the sofa, her hands clasped in front of her chest. Reina walked into the living room from the kitchen, a saucer with a teacup in her hands. She placed the saucer on the table in front of Kisho, then she sat beside Rose.

The group waited in silence, anxious to hear Kisho's assessment. Despite the storm of thoughts clouding his mind, the man remained calm. He leaned forward, grabbed the teacup, then he took a sip—calm, composed, *ready*.

Eager, Rose said, "Well? What happened in there?" Kisho returned the cup to the saucer. Rose asked, "It's an incubus, isn't it? It's either a very powerful incubus pretending to be Richard or Richard somehow became an incubus after he died, right? I swear, I could feel it from the moment I arrived. It wasn't spiritual energy, but there was so much... so much *sexual* energy in this place. I was correct, right?"

Kisho said, "Yes."

Reina stuttered, "Can–Can this incubus-thing possess people?"

"It's certainly a possibility. When it comes to the supernatural, the rules aren't exactly set in stone. I suppose you can say the same about human nature."

Edmund stopped pacing, He wagged his index finger at Kisho and said, "Listen, I'm not like you or Rose. I'm not... connected to the supernatural world or whatever you'd like to call it. But I believe in it and I've seen things I don't think I'll ever be able to explain. I have a 'feeling,' too, and I've had this 'feeling' since we first interacted with Julie. What about the others, Kisho? There are other entities inside of her, right? Don't tell me you haven't felt it. She must be possessed by more."

Kisho stared at Edmund with curious eyes. *We're all connected to the supernatural world,* he thought, *without us, there would be no such thing as supernatural.* He didn't want to correct the man, though. In fact, he wanted to applaud him for speaking up. Edmund was a rational man—a businessman—but he had an open mind and a big heart.

Kisho said, "You're correct as well." He straightened his legs and leaned forward, his elbows on his knees. He explained, "This is my theory. As Rose explained, I believe Julie is being attacked by an incubus. This incubus might actually be Richard Knight or it might just be posing as the man to weaken Julie's resolve. If I had to bet, I'd be willing to wager the incubus is Richard. Regardless, the demon's main goal is strange: he wants to impregnate Julie in order to bring about the birth of evil. In a sense, this would reincarnate him while forever tormenting Julie. If he can't do that, well... He wants to hurt as many people as possible, including the young woman."

The group was awed by Kisho's theory. Reina held her trembling hands over her mouth as she whimpered. Rose rubbed Reina's shoulder, trying her best to comfort her.

Shocked, Edmund stared at the floor and said, "Christ, imagine that. A dead father impregnates his own daughter so he can be reborn as her evil son..."

Kisho continued, "There's more. I believe Richard has opened a door—so to speak—allowing other wandering spirits and demons to walk through."

Reina shook her head and asked, "What does that even mean?"

"The earthly realm and the spirit realm work hand-in-hand. One does not exist without the other. Richard has made Julie into a beacon and a gate. Every demonic force can feel her innocent presence, so they're naturally drawn to her. Think of Julie as a magnet. She is attracting hundreds of evil spirits, and that includes her father and a horde of incubi. They come to her, then they walk through the gate, allowing them to take control of Julie's body. Layman's terms, of course."

Reina was baffled by the explanation. She didn't understand most of Kisho's theory. *How can a girl be turned into a beacon and a gate?*–she thought. The expression on her face read: *what the hell are you talking about?* She understood enough, though. Her daughter was possessed by demons and evil spirits— and she was in grave danger.

Reina asked, "How do we get rid of them? Hmm? How do we save Julie?"

Kisho responded, "I wasn't really able to talk to your daughter when I entered the room. I spoke to spirits and I saw demons. I'm curious: what are your daughter's beliefs?"

"Does that matter?"

"Possibly not, but I'd like to know as much about Julie as possible before I proceed."

Reluctant, Reina said, "I'm... I'm not completely sure. We're not a very religious family. I believe in God—*a* God—but I don't go to church. I don't follow a bible or anything like that. I just believe in... in something. Julie is the same, I guess. The few times we ever spoke about it, she claimed she believed in God, but sometimes she wasn't sure. I guess she's agnostic. I don't know, I just don't know."

Kisho carefully examined Reina's demeanor. The woman appeared regretful, as if she did something wrong. In his eyes, it wasn't a sin to live with doubt. The world was filled with more questions than answers after all.

Kisho said, "An exorcism might work. I could perform it myself, too. However, a traditional exorcism would be difficult to execute. It wouldn't mean much without the official backing of the church. And, since Julie is agnostic, it also might *not* work."

Reina cried, "This is why I didn't want to tell you. I knew you'd abandon us for the chu-"

"I'm not abandoning you," Kisho interrupted. "Like I said, an exorcism could work, but it might not be effective. It might not be necessary, either. I don't believe a traditional demon is possessing Julie. I believe Richard is the problem. If we can expel Richard, we might be able to close the gate."

In an uncertain tone, Rose said, "So, we just get rid of the incubus while hundreds of other entities are trying to tear her apart?"

Kisho nodded.

Reina asked, "How? If you won't perform the exorcism, how do we stop the incubus?"

Kisho explained, "This is Julie's battle, Ms. Knight. She must take a stand against the incubus since the incubus draws its strength from her. While taking her stand, she must be firm, dedicated, and honest. Her rejection must come from the heart."

"It sounds like something from a movie," Edmund said. "Turn your back on the bogeyman and he loses his power."

"I suppose you can think of it like that. However, she can't just turn her back on him. She must tell her father to leave without a hint of doubt in her mind or heart. In turn, she would be accepting the good and the bad of her history with her father while expelling him from her mind. That is very important: she must accept that her father was a bad man, she must accept that she did nothing wrong, then she must send him back from where he came."

Reina asked, "Are you telling me she has to... to forgive her father's abuse?"

Kisho shook his head and said, "*Accept*. Her mind is clouded with guilt, shame, doubt... everything. Although it may not be on purpose, she is empowering her father by trying to avoid him. She knows she's possessed, so she's hiding. And, she's hiding because of her feelings. Acceptance and forgiveness are not the same. Accepting the past simply means she can start moving forward."

Yet again, the living room was dominated by silence. Reina, Rose, and Edmund lowered their heads and stared down. Kisho made it sound as if there wasn't much they could do in the situation. A grim atmosphere, cold and eerie, settled over them.

Kisho said, "If Julie believes in anything, this is her best time to vanish the spirits through prayer." He stared at Reina and said, "I think it would be best if you prayed, too."

Chiming in, Reina asked, "If this is Julie's battle, how do we let her know that? She can't keep hiding forever, right? Someone needs to tell her what she has to do, *right?*"

Kisho responded, "Yes. It may be difficult to accept, but we must wait."

"For what?"

"We must wait until Richard attacks her again..."

Reina's heart sank upon hearing his suggestion. She held her hand over her chest and leaned back in her seat, disoriented. Short, panicked breaths escaped her lips. Tears welled in her eyes. *Let your daughter suffer*—a mother couldn't easily agree to that.

Reina cried, "No, no, no... I can't watch that again. Please, don't let him hurt her again. No, God, no..."

As he gazed into Reina's eyes, Kisho said, "I'm afraid it's the only way. From what you've told me and from what I've seen, it is the only time where Julie is herself for a prolonged period. It is also the only time Richard is not hiding inside of her. She will be with us... and *he* will be vulnerable."

Reina gazed back into Kisho's eyes. She couldn't spot a shred of deceit in his soul. The man's intentions were pure. She glanced over at Rose, then at Edmund. The parapsychologists didn't offer any alternative solutions to the situation, but they were prepared to support Reina and her family until the very end.

Rose turned her attention to Kisho. Teary-eyed, she bit her bottom lip and nodded, communicating through the gesture—*okay, I trust you.* Kisho smiled and returned the nod, as if to say: *thank you, I won't let you down.*

Chapter Nineteen

The Liberation of Julie Knight

Eighteen hours passed since Kisho's first interview. The day came and went, and nighttime arrived with a roaring downpour. The windows rattled with each powerful gust of wind. Aside from the natural ruckus, the home was quiet. It felt as if the home were abandoned by the neighborhood. Words of comfort were not shared during the somber hours, either. The occupants kept to themselves, waiting for the inevitable attack.

Reina and Rose sat on the sofa in the living room. Kisho stood nearby, staring out a window as rain cascaded down the glass. Edmund leaned on a kitchen counter as he sipped his coffee, struggling to tame his jitters. Nick sat on his bed and stared at the door, locked in his bedroom and surrounded by a feeling of despair.

A cold sensation swept across all of them—an icy chill, like the chill of death. They had spent the day ignoring Julie's generic cries. They heard several voices coming from Julie's bedroom. Obscenities emerged from her room and echoed through the house. The restless spirits were craving attention. The voices belonged to Ted Hall and Marie Brooks—among others—but they were insignificant. They needed to hear Julie's voice, her *real* voice, in order to proceed.

The house became silent for a minute—no voices, no groans, no creaks. Then, a bloodcurdling shriek echoed through the home. Reina and Rose glanced over at the hall. With his hands clasped behind his back, Kisho turned around. Edmund peeked around the corner of the archway, frightened. Nick stood from his bed, ready to run at the first sign of trouble.

Kisho said, "It's time. Remember the plan."

The group simultaneously nodded in agreement. Kisho marched to the bedroom and the group followed him. He moved the latch lock, opened the door, then he stepped into the room.

Julie writhed on the bed, weeping and panting. Her pajama bottoms were pulled down to her ankles and her legs were separated, revealing her bare crotch. The bottom half of the mattress appeared to be sunken, as if someone were sitting between Julie's legs. The bed rocked on its own, too, banging on the neighboring wall while screeching across the floorboards.

Julie glanced over at the door and yelled, "Mom! Help! Help me! Mom, *please!*"

Reina pushed Kisho aside and ran to her daughter's side. She stopped beside the bed, carefully examining her daughter and the mattress. She could feel the malevolent presence in the room—evil in its purest form.

Rosy-cheeked, Reina shouted, "Richard, you sick bastard! Get away from her! This is about me, isn't it? You want me, don't you? Then take me! I'm here, you fucking animal! I'm still here! Come–"

Reina was struck in the face, her left cheek deflating and her hair swinging to the right. She had felt a similar hit before—a savage backhanded slap. The unexpected blow caused her to fall to her knees in front of the computer desk. She rubbed her cheek as she stared up at the bed—it stopped rocking. The plan worked.

Reina was the bait. She was willing to sacrifice herself in order to buy time for the rest of the group.

Fueled by her hatred for her deceased husband, Reina scowled and said, "You're a coward, Richard. You're a pathetic asshole. You stupid, insecure, small-dicked asshole... You hear me, don't you?"

She was struck again, launching her from the floor and hurling her at the desk. The monitor and the computer tipped over as she clashed with the desk. She remained defiant, though. She continued to attack her husband with every insult she could imagine. Although his body died a decade ago, his ego was still alive and vulnerable.

While Reina fought with Richard's spirit, Kisho, Rose, and Edmund rushed to the bed. Rose unlocked the two handcuffs on one side of the bed while Edmund unlocked the others.

As the parapsychologists worked, Kisho leaned closer to Julie's ear and whispered, "Julie, this is a life-or-death situation. It's time to act. In order to cleanse your soul—to expel the spirits and demons who have possessed your body—you must *vanquish* your father. He must be defeated."

Julie stared into Kisho's eyes, scared and confused. She lifted her pants up to her waist, then she rubbed her sore wrists. She was hurt, tired, and afraid, but she trusted the group. For the first time in weeks, she was able to control her body.

She glanced over at the other end of the room. Her mother was pinned to the wall, her feet hovering a foot over the floor. She gasped as Reina was repeatedly slapped. Richard cycled between arms, hitting her with lefts and rights. It looked like Reina was shaking her head with each violent slap.

Determined, Julie turned towards Kisho and asked, "*How?* How do I beat him?"

Kisho explained, "You must admit to the abuse he inflicted upon you. You must acknowledge that you are the victim and you are not guilty of anything. You must remember the good and the bad, then you must *erase* those memories from your mind. And, all of your actions must be genuine."

"You–You want me to... to erase my father from my memories? You want me to forget the bad... and the good? He was my dad, mister. He–He wasn't always a bad guy, I swear. He was... He was my dad."

Teary-eyed, Julie looked up at the ceiling and reminisced about the past. Her mind was flooded with memories from her childhood. She remembered the good times—the birthday parties, the visits to the park, the games, *the love.* By erasing the good, she felt like she would be making her father into a villain, and no child ever wanted to do that.

Kisho pointed at Reina and said, "This is your last chance."

Julie looked over at her mother. She grimaced and whimpered, appalled by the violence. Although she cherished the good memories of her father, she realized he died as a bad person and his spirit did not change. She groaned as she staggered to her feet. Her legs wobbled under her, forcing her to lean on a bedpost.

She shouted, "Stop! Stop it, dad!" Reina cried as the beating continued. Julie stomped and yelled, "Stop it, you bastard!"

The beating stopped with the shout. Reina, out of

breath, fell to her knees near the desk. She coughed and grunted as she pushed her tousled hair aside. Rose ran to her side. She rubbed her cheeks and swiped at her hair, awed by the attack. Kisho and Edmund examined the room, searching for the entity, but to no avail—there was no one in sight.

To the untrained eye, it appeared as if Julie were screaming at a wall. However, the young woman could see her nude father in the room. The grizzled, black-eyed man stood over Reina. He stared at his daughter, surprised by her sudden surge in confidence.

Eyes brimming with tears, Julie said, "You bastard... You ruined my life. I loved you. I loved you so much, dad. You were everything to me. I didn't care about the presents or the trips, I cared about *you* and your *words* and your *heart*. You made me feel so loved. Then... you took me to the bathroom and you... you made me take a bath with you. You said it was normal. 'It's natural, sweetie,' that's what you said. I trusted you and you... you broke that trust. You did nasty things to me. I thought it was my fault for so long, but I know now: I'm *not* responsible and it's okay to hate you. I don't have to protect your image anymore, not for me or anyone else. I'm done with you."

The room became quiet after Julie's powerful speech. The parapsychologists glanced at each other, baffled. Reina looked at her daughter, then at Kisho. Kisho stared up at the ceiling. Julie couldn't see her father anymore, either. He vanished after she blinked.

Julie said, "I did what you said. Is it–"

She gasped upon feeling a set of hands on her waist. Her eyes widened as she levitated a meter above the bed. She glanced back at her group of rescuers, searching for a sense of reassurance. Everyone in the room stared back at her, eyes and mouths wide open.

Julie shrieked as she was thrown to the floor beside the bed. Before she could say another word, she was dragged out of the room. She tried to grab the doorway, but her grip was too weak and the entity was too strong.

Reina stumbled forward and shouted, "Julie!"

The door slammed on its own, then the locks turned.

***

The bedroom was swallowed by a wave of darkness. Only a slit of light entered the room through the gap under the door thanks to the light in the hallway.

Kisho twisted the lock and turned the knob, but the door wouldn't budge. Edmund rammed the door with his shoulder, but his efforts were fruitless. They were locked in the room by a spiritual force.

Reina shouted, "Open the door! We have to help her, damn it!"

Frustrated, Edmund yelled, "It's locked for Christ's sake! It's jammed!"

"Damn it, we have to help my baby! Please, open the door. Please..."

As Edmund continued to ram the door, Kisho leaned closer to the doorway and shouted, "Julie! Julie, you must get rid of the good and the bad! Don't let him manipulate you, don't let him win! He is *not* the man you remember! He hasn't been that man in a long time!"

Julie's cries echoed through the home, emerging

from the living room. During the chaos, she couldn't hear all of Kisho's advice.

A soft giggle emerged in the room—*devious laughter.* Kisho, Edmund, Reina, and Rose slowly turned around. The giggling continued, emerging from the farthest corner of the room away from the door. Rose and Reina looked at each other, then they glanced over at Kisho and Edmund. Rose nodded at the men, as if to say: *get that door open, we'll handle this.*

Kisho and Edmund understood Rose's plan. The men tackled the door with all of their might, trying their best to create an escape route.

With trembling hands, Reina pulled her cell phone out of her robe pocket. She opened the flashlight app, she took a deep breath in an attempt to control herself, then she illuminated the room with the camera's flash. Like a wet bar of soap in the shower, the phone slipped and slid in her hands as she spotted the source of the laughter.

A roly-poly woman—short and round—stood in the corner of the room. Webs of thick blue veins protruded from the woman's gray, coarse skin. Dressed like an infant, she wore a blue bonnet, a white bob, and a large diaper. Her frizzy grizzled hair was tucked into the hat. Green puke, resembling pea soup, dribbled across her chin and stained her bib. A white liquid appeared to be oozing out of her large, wrinkly breasts. She held a baby bottle in one hand and a voodoo doll in the other.

Awed by her appearance, Reina muttered, "Who the hell is that?"

Edmund and Kisho glanced back. Kisho narrowed his eyes as he examined the woman while Edmund hopped and gasped upon spotting her.

As the thought dawned on him, Edmund stuttered, "Tha–That's Marie Brooks."

"The voodoo killer," Rose whispered. She stepped forward and shouted, "Get that door open, Ed! And keep that light on, Ms. Knight!"

In a soft, bubbly voice, Marie asked, "Did you come to play with me, miss?"

Rose said, "In the name of Jesus Christ and everything holy, we ask for protection from the evil spirits and entities in this house..."

"You're praying?" Marie said in an uncertain tone. "Mama used to pray, too, miss. She's dead now."

Rose continued, "We ask for peace, light, and righteousness during our darkest time. We also ask for strength—the strength to overcome our vices and to block out the evil. Amen."

"You're praying... *against me?* You're not nice, lady. You're just another bully, aren't you? You're just like Billy!"

"Marie Brooks, we mean you no harm. There is no ill-will in my body. I do *not* hate you, I do *not* fear you. You are dead, and that is a fact. This is not your world anymore. You can move on now. You can do it peacefully. I can help you, okay?"

Marie narrowed her eyes and tilted her head, as if she were confused. She stepped forward, the floorboards groaning under her weight. Reina took two steps back as she watched the confrontation, cautious and terrified.

Rose stood her ground, though. She didn't show fear around the lost spirit. Marie grinned, then she hit her with a backhanded slap. Rose lurched towards the foot of the bed, caught off guard by the blow. She cried as she rubbed her jaw. She felt like she was hit with a brick.

With a deadpan expression, Marie said, "You're just a bully like everyone else. I *hate* bullies. I hate them so much. I know how to take care of them, though. Mama taught me a long time ago... then I taught her how to die." She simpered, then she said, "I'll teach all of you, too."

Reina stepped in reverse until her back hit the wall near the door. She felt like death was on the horizon, but she didn't fear for her own safety. She could only think about Julie and the challenges she was facing in the living room. *I'm sorry, sweetie,* she thought, *I failed you.*

Edmund pulled Reina to the door. He said, "You help Kisho and I'll help Rose. Go." He rushed to Rose's side, then he dragged her away from the foot of the bed—barely dodging a kick from Marie. As he helped Rose to her feet, Edmund said, "Just like old times, huh?"

Rose wiped the tears from her cheeks and said, "Yeah, just like old times."

"And just like old times, we're going to cleanse this house and get out of here—alive and maybe a little richer."

The couple chuckled. They turned their attention to Marie, ready to exorcise the spirit. Meanwhile, Kisho kicked at the doorknob while Reina tossed her body at the door. The room was hectic, the odds were stacked against them, but the battle wasn't over. A glimmer of hope still sparkled in the abyss.

***

Nick hid under his covers with his hands over his ears and his eyes squeezed shut. He heard his sister's bloodcurdling shriek as she was dragged to the living room. He heard the incessant banging on the door as the adults tried to escape Julie's bedroom. The weeping and the screaming paralyzed him. Hopeless and helpless, he whimpered under the covers as he struggled to muster the courage to move.

He thought: *do I go out there and help her by myself? Do I grab mom's gun and shoot her like she said?* He sniveled and shook his head. He couldn't accept the idea of killing his own sister. It was impossible.

Nick whispered, "I can't... I'm sorry, Julie. I just can't do it. I'm scared. I'm so–"

The sound of a creaky floorboard emerged in the room. The everyday noise was louder than usual, shrill and ominous. The sound seeped past his hands and drilled into his ears, causing him to shudder, as if he had heard a key scraping glass. The creaky sound occurred again, quickly followed by the same noise. Someone was walking towards his bed—but his door was locked.

Nick's breathing intensified as the sound grew louder. He gritted his teeth and frantically shook his head. One thought rattled in his skull: *this isn't happening, this isn't happening.*

He emerged from under the covers and shouted, "This isn't happening! It's not real!"

He opened his eyes and glanced around. The room was dark and empty. The banging, screaming, and crying stopped.

Nick stuttered, "He–Hello? Is... Is anyone there?"

The room remained quiet. Before he could say another word, the mattress shook, causing him to sway from side to side. As the frame settled, a childish simper emerged from under the bed. The soft laughter was eerie considering the circumstances.

Nick grabbed his cell phone from the neighboring nightstand. He wiped the sweat from his brow with the back of his hand, then he swiped at his nose. He struggled to keep his composure. As he breathed heavily, he thought: *I can do this, there's no such thing as the bogeyman.*

He leaned over the edge of the bed, moving a centimeter per second—slow, vigilant, and calculated. As he illuminated the area under his bed, the boy gasped and fell to the floor.

Julie hid under the bed, curled in a ball like a sleeping dog. She wasn't the same, though. Her skin was milky white, smooth and unblemished. Her hair was clean and straight. Her eyes glimmered with innocence, like a child who hadn't yet been tainted by the filthy world. She only wore a push-up bra and matching lace panties. With a seductive stare, she licked her lips and leered at her brother.

Nick stuttered, "Wha–What are you doing here, Julie? How did you... What's going on?"

Julie responded, "I'm feeling better now, Nicky. I thought we should celebrate."

"Celebrate?"

"Yes, *celebrate.*"

Julie reached out from under the bed. She rubbed Nick's thigh as she sucked on her index finger. She even moaned to tease him. Nick gasped and rapidly blinked. He was a thirteen-year-old boy, he was interested in sex, but he was baffled and disgusted by his sister's behavior. He scooted a foot back.

He asked, "What are you doing?"

"I just want to play, Nick. Don't you want to play

with your big sister? Hmm? I think you do, sweetie. Listen up: let's play a naughty game, okay? A game with no rules, no judgment, *no consequences.* You can do anything to me and I can do *anything* to you. Does that sound good to you? I bet it does..."

Nick shook his head. The woman under his bed resembled his sister, but she was clearly something different. She was an apparition—an entity of evil.

Teary-eyed, Nick asked, "Did... Did you die?"

Julie huffed, then she said, "Of course not, baby. How could I be talking to you if I died? I'm alive and I'm healthy, and it's all thanks to you and your support. Let me thank you for that, sweetie. Come here."

She crawled out from under the bed. On her knees, she leaned forward and gently stroked Nick's thigh. She giggled as she felt the boy's soft trembling. He couldn't easily bury his natural teenage urges after all. Nick grimaced as he stared down at Julie's hand. He was simultaneously excited and scared. He didn't know what to think or how to feel.

Nick tightly closed his eyes and whispered, "*No.* You're not real. You should be hurt. There should be bruises on–on your face and wrists. You should look... *sick.* This isn't you. It's impossible."

"I'm real, baby..."

"No, you're not. You never called me 'baby' before. You're not real. It's all in my head. It's all in my head..."

In a gruff tone, a man said, "I *am* real, boy."

Nick opened his eyes. He gasped and crawled back upon spotting a greasy, middle-aged man sitting in front of him—*Ted Hall.* He only wore white briefs, revealing his beer belly and flabby breasts. The man cackled as he swiped at his thinning hair and smirked. He smacked his lips as he looked lasciviously at the boy. He appeared to be pitching a tent, too.

Ted said, "Let's play 'hide the sausage in the corn hole.' How about it, kiddo? You up for it?"

Wide-eyed, Nick staggered to his feet and yelled, "Mom!"

As Ted giggled, Nick rushed out of the room and skidded to a stop in the hallway. The ruckus in the house returned with full force. He could hear the struggle in Julie's bedroom, he heard his sister crying in the living room. His heart told him to help, but his instincts told him to survive.

The boy dashed into his mother's bedroom. He closed the door behind him, then he sighed in relief. He fell to his knees beside his mother's bed, then he pulled a black case from under the bed—a pistol case. He carried the case in his arms as he ran into the closet. He pushed the coats and shoe boxes aside, then he sat on the closet floor. He closed the doors and peeked through the blinds.

Although the lights were off, Nick could still see into the room. He sat with his knees up to his face, the pistol case clenched between his legs and chest. He shivered and whimpered, his mind flooded with hundreds of thoughts. He thought about his sister's request: *kill me.* He believed her death would end the nightmare for everyone, but he wasn't ready to proceed.

In the room, hidden in the shadows, Ted Hall said, "Come out, Nicky. I want to play a naughty, *naughty* game with you. Come on, let's have some fun, boy."

Nick lowered his head and sobbed. The door remained closed, but Ted somehow lurked inside of the bedroom.

Tears dripping from his eyes like raindrops, Nick whispered, "Please don't hurt me. Don't hurt my mom. Don't hurt my sister. Don't make me do this. I... I don't want to kill her. I just want this to end..."

***

Julie shrieked as she slid across the floor, her filthy fingernails scraping the floorboards. She grabbed the leg of a console table in the hallway, but to no avail—the table was dragged with her. She lost her grip and released the table. She tried to scratch the floor, but her fingernails *cracked* and *snapped* off due to the sheer force of the entity's pull.

She turned on her back and stared up as she reached the living room. She could finally see her attacker again. Richard Knight held her ankles and dragged her to the center of the living room. Huffing and puffing, the man was visibly furious. His daughter was equally enraged—like father, like daughter.

As Richard released her right ankle, Julie kicked her father's crotch. She felt his groin on her bare foot, he was tangible, but the kick didn't hurt him. So, she kicked him again and again, but her efforts were fruitless.

Richard chuckled, then he said, "You stupid cunt, you're just as dumb as your whore mother." He released her other leg, then he walked over her body. As he struck her with a barrage of backhanded slaps, the wicked man shouted, "Don't ever insult me again, girl! You... show... some... *goddamn...* respect to your father!"

Julie wrapped her arms around her head, trying to block the powerful slaps. Despite her efforts, a few of her father's strikes still slipped past her arms and hit her face. If he couldn't hit her face, he would gladly beat her arms anyway. Each hit stung like alcohol and lemon poured into a fresh wound. She had never felt such a brutal beating.

She cried, "Stop! Please, daddy, stop it!"

Richard grabbed a fistful of her hair and said, "I need to teach you a lesson, girl. This'll end as soon as you learn to respect me."

He threw her onto the coffee table. The laptops and cameras fell to the floor as the glass coffee table shattered into dozens of sharp shards—some small, some large. The shards stabbed Julie's arms, chest, and face. Shards of all shapes and sizes protruded from her flesh. Some of the shards were even trapped deep in the gashes. Blood streamed across her cheeks, neck, and forearms.

Julie trembled as she tried to stand, the glass crackling under her palms and knees. She didn't have the opportunity to recompose herself.

Richard grabbed another fistful of her hair, then he lifted her limp body from the ground. As she coughed and grunted, he hurled her across the room. *Thud*—her head clashed with a brick on the fireplace. She was immediately dazed by the blow, barely clinging to her consciousness. The room spinning around her, she fell to the floor in front of the fireplace.

Disoriented, she mumbled, "What... What happened?"

Her vision was blurred by the devastating blow. She felt a numb, tingling sensation in her head. She couldn't feel the blood leaking from the side of her head, though. She could, however, feel her pants slipping down her legs. She could also feel the fear pumping through her veins. *It's happening again,* she thought, *he won't stop until I make him stop.*

She grabbed the waistband of her pants and stopped Richard from disrobing her. She held her breath as she crawled forward, exerting all of the energy she could muster. She staggered to her knees, then she turned towards her father. She was covered in blood due to the vicious beating, but she wasn't ready to quit.

Leaning on the fireplace, Julie stood to her feet and said, "You can't... You can't hurt me anymore. You don't have the... the power to do that. You're not my father. You stopped being my father after we went into that bathroom. You... You're just a bastard. I'm ready to let you go."

Richard clenched his jaw as he glared at his daughter. The man was visibly upset. Yet, he couldn't attack her. The words were hurting him—and Julie realized that.

Julie said, "That's right. It wasn't my fault. You're *not* my father. And I'm ready to let you go!"

With the passionate declaration, all of the doors in the house swung open. Kisho and Reina staggered back, caught off guard by the sudden opening. Edmund and Rose glanced over at the door, then back at Marie Brooks—the apparition vanished. From the closet, Nick watched as the door opened on its own, but he couldn't see Ted Hall. The boy stayed in the closet. He opened the case and began loading the gun. He prepared himself for the worst possible scenario.

Kisho, Reina, Rose, and Edmund ran to the living room. The group was shocked by the destruction in the room as well as Julie's bloodied condition. They could see Richard again, too. The man appeared faint, though, as if he were slowly vanishing.

Richard said, "You belong to me, you little whore. You ruined my life and now you want to ruin my afterlife? *No.* You're mine. Mine! If you won't have my baby... then I'll just have to kill you all."

The group glanced over at the front door as the locks twisted and turned, sealing them in the house. The entire home began to tremble. The sound of wood groaning and cracking echoed through the house. The lights flickered until the bulbs exploded. It felt as if the house would collapse at any moment, crushing and killing everyone inside.

Struggling to keep his balance, Kisho lurched to Julie's side. He grabbed her shoulders and shouted, "You must finish it!"

Julie cried, "I'm trying! I'm... I'm really trying. I hurt him, but he won't leave. I just don't know what else to do. I can't keep going. I'm sorry, we... we lost."

"Julie, I know you're scared, but you have to keep fighting. We can't hurt him for you, but you're not alone. We can see him, too. *I* can see him."

"You–You can?"

"Yes. The nude man. He has wavy hair, stubble on his jaw, and black eyes. I see him. You're not alone. You can finish this."

Eyes glimmering with hope, Julie smiled as she looked at Kisho. For the first time in weeks, she felt like she wasn't alone. Her family witnessed the impossible, but they never saw Richard in his human form. She wasn't trapped in a nightmare, she wasn't hallucinating in an insane asylum. Her hope was rekindled by Kisho's sincere words and benign heart.

Julie asked, "What do I do? I already did what you told me to do. What's next?"

Kisho explained, "You've rejected your father and you were genuine. I can feel that. Something else is keeping him bound to you and the human realm. There must be some sort of remnant of your father that you haven't gotten rid of... A powerful symbol of his past love..."

Julie's eyes widened. She said, "I know what it is." As she ran to her room, she shouted, "Light the fireplace! I'll be back!"

The light bulbs in the corridor exploded as she sprinted down the hall. Dark, distorted faces appeared on the walls. The faces were warped—gaping mouths, drooping cheeks, and hollow eyes—as if they were screaming in agony. Ghastly moans escaped their gaping mouths, reverberating with the sound of cracking wood. The faces belonged to the spirits who were attached to Julie's mind.

Julie ignored the cries, though. She teetered left-and-right as the floor trembled, but she didn't stop moving. She stumbled into the bedroom and fell to her knees beside the foot of the bed, as if she were about to pray before sleeping. She reached under the bed and pulled out an old, dusty shoe box. She tossed the lid aside, then she sighed.

A threadbare teddy bear and a letter in an envelope were stored in the box. The teddy bear was a gift from her father—the best gift she ever received. Her father wrote the letter when she was five years old, before the drugs and alcohol consumed him. Reina had convinced Richard to write Julie a letter every year to create a strong father-daughter bond. That was the last letter he ever gave her.

Julie, refusing to touch the gifts, placed the lid on the box and whispered, "I'm done with you."

She stumbled back into the living room, barely keeping her balance. Glass crackled under her feet as she ran to the fireplace. Leaving bloody footprints with each step, the young woman ignored the pain from the lacerations on her soles. She had experienced much worse during the horrifying possession of her body. She slid to a stop next to Kisho in front of the fireplace.

"Wait!" Richard shouted.

Julie stopped before she could throw the box into the fire. She glanced over her shoulder, eyes glistening with tears. Her father stood at the center of the room. He appeared normal—he wore clean clothes and his eyes were no longer black. He even smiled. He resembled the man from her most pleasant memories.

In a soft tone, Richard said, "Don't do this, sweetie. If you do this, you'll never see me again. *Never.* You realize that, don't you? You have an opportunity most people don't get. You can reconnect with your dead father. Do you know how many children would love to see their dead parents again? Don't do this, Julie. *Please.*"

Julie gazed into her father's eyes, lost in memories of happiness. As the home continued to tremble, Reina, Rose, and Edmund stared at Julie with furrowed brows. They couldn't see or hear Richard, so they could only watch as Julie inexplicably hesitated. Kisho experienced the entire confrontation, but he did not interfere.

It was Julie's battle.

Tears trickling from her eyes with each blink, Julie said, "You can't fool me anymore, dad. You're a... a monster. You died a monster and you stayed a monster. I don't want to see you anymore. I don't love you anymore."

Richard said, "Julie, wait. I can change. I'm not–" As Julie tossed the box into the fireplace, Richard shouted, "No!"

The shaking grew stronger as the gifts burned. The floorboards cracked and separated, leaving a one-foot wide gap in the living room. The ceiling in the kitchen cracked, then it collapsed. The windows rattled, then the glass shattered.

Julie and the adults cowered in the corner of the room. Reina and Rose wrapped their arms around Julie while Kisho and Edmund used their bodies to cover the women. Nick still hid in the bedroom, crying as he held the loaded pistol in his trembling hands.

After a minute of shaking, the quake ended. The house became silent. Reina glanced around the living room, astonished by the destruction.

She stuttered, "I–Is it over?"

Julie emerged from under the adults. She looked every which way, searching for any signs of her father's survival. Richard, the lost spirits, and the demons vanished during the tremor.

Tears of joy streaming across her cheeks, Julie grimaced and cried, "It's over. It's finally over."

Chapter Twenty

The End

Reina and Julie sat on the sofa, watching as the flames in the fireplace danced. Julie rested her head on her mother's shoulder while Reina caressed her daughter's hair. Rose swept the broken glass with a broom while Edmund salvaged the equipment. Kisho stood near the fireplace, his hands on his hips. The home was finally peaceful.

As she stroked her daughter's cheek, Reina said, "We're going to have to get you to a hospital for all of these cuts and bruises... God, it looks so bad."

Julie responded, "It doesn't hurt so much."

"That's good, but we're still going. We should get you cleaned up, though. A warm shower or bath should help. It always helped me when I was stressed. Are... Are you sure you're feeling better now? Is everything okay here?"

Julie glanced around the room and said, "I think so. I don't feel 'it' anymore. I don't feel *him* anymore. I think everything's going to be okay." She looked at Rose and Edmund. She asked, "You're from that show, aren't you? Unearthly Happenings, right?"

Rose smiled and said, "Yup. That's us."

Julie frowned upon noticing the marks on Rose's face. Her saviors were clearly beaten during the rescue.

Julie said, "You're hurt because of me. I'm sorry."

"Oh, there's no need to apologize. We're just glad to help," Rose responded.

"Thank you. Um... Since you're here, does that mean I'm going to be on your show? Are you... Are you going to use me?"

Still smiling, Rose said, "I think we can skip this episode, Julie."

"No, I... I don't think that's necessary. I mean, I know you blur everyone's faces anyway. I just... If it helps other people like me, I want to share my story. It's okay."

Edmund grinned from ear-to-ear and said, "Well, it's settled. Thank you, darling."

Rose playfully slapped his chest and giggled. The group shared a laugh, shrugging off Edmund's innocent greed. Julie glanced over at Kisho, who chuckled softly near the fireplace.

Julie said, "I didn't get your name."

"It's Kisho Sato, miss"

"Kisho Sato... Thank you for understanding me. Thank you for saving me."

"It was my pleasure. Your mother, Rose, and Edmund helped more than you can possibly imagine, too. They deserve your gratitude. Me? Well, I'm just a... a wanderer. I go where I'm needed."

Julie was impressed by the man's eloquence. He was confident, generous, and gentle. He was a real hero.

She asked, "Is there anything else I should know?"

Kisho responded, "I believe this is over. You will obviously have to recover due to your physical and mental wounds, but you will survive. You may also experience some *supernatural* visions, for lack of a better term. You may see spirits, but they won't be able to harm you."

Concerned, Reina asked, "How long will she see

them?"

"It could be days, weeks, months, years... Let me put it this way: my supernatural journey started when I was possessed four decades ago—and I'm still seeing spirits today. I'm fine, though. If you're ever concerned, you can always give me a call."

The sound of creaky floorboards interrupted the conversation. The group simultaneously glanced over at the hallway. The relief and joy were wiped from their faces.

Rosy-cheeked, Nick stood in the hallway. Trembling, he held the loaded gun with both hands and aimed at the couch. His finger sat on the trigger, ready to shoot at the first sign of trouble. He sniffled and wiped his tears on his shoulder, trying to remain strong.

Reina stuttered, "N–Nick, what... what are you doing, baby?" She tightly closed her eyes and shook her head. She said, "I forgot about you... I ignored you. Is that what this is about? I'm sorry, sweetie. There was just so much on–"

"Are you really her?" Nick interrupted, his voice cracking.

Reina asked, "What are you talking about?"

"Not you. *Julie.* Is... Is that really Julie?"

The adults looked at each other with raised brows. Julie emerged from behind her mother's shoulder. She could see the fear and pain in her brother's eyes.

Nick wagged the gun and said, "You told me to shoot you if things got out of control." He glanced around, examining the destroyed property and battered adults. He said, "Things got out of control. This is what you told me to do. I... I have to shoot you."

Julie stood up with her hands over her head, as if

she were caught by the police. She said, "I'm okay now, Nick. I'm back to normal. I won't be able to hurt anyone anymore. I can't hurt you, mom, or even myself because I don't want to. It's over. We won."

"Are... Are you lying to me?"

"No. I could never lie to you. You're my brother and I love you. I'm better now, squirt."

For a moment, Nick strongly considered pulling the trigger. He couldn't tell if the situation was real or fake. In his bedroom, Ted Hall's spirit was able to manipulate his perception. *Is it happening again?*–he thought. One word convinced him that his sister had returned, though: *squirt.*

Nick grimaced as he lowered the gun. He carefully placed the pistol on the floor, then he ran into his sister's arms. The pair embraced, whimpering and groaning. Reina joined the hug, too. They sat together on the sofa, closer than ever before. Reina scolded her son for taking her handgun, Nick apologized for his actions, and Julie felt nothing but love around her family. The others shared a sigh of relief.

As she recomposed herself, Julie sniffled and asked, "Are all of you staying?"

Edmund joked, "Why? Need us to clean up the mess?"

Julie laughed, then she said, "No, no. I... I just think it would be nice if you stuck around."

"I can't," Kisho responded. "Your journey ends here, but mine continues elsewhere. I have been requested to aid a family at a hotel in Japan."

Rose furrowed her brow and asked, "Really? Which one?"

"It's a little hotel in Tokyo. It's bustling with supernatural activity and some of it has been harmful to a few people. I can't share more at the moment, though. It wouldn't be appropriate."

"Interesting. Well, if you need a hand, let us know. Maybe we can join you when we're done here."

Eyes glowing with hope, Julie asked, "Does that mean you're staying?"

"Yep. Ed and I will stick around for a few days. I just want to make sure you're all okay—mentally and physically. We'll even help you clean up this mess... Well, you might actually have to move."

As she glanced over at the kitchen, Reina said, "You're right. We definitely won't be having breakfast here. Let's get cleaned up, then we can go to a diner. Okay?" As she helped her daughter stand, Reina said, "I'd really be honored if you stuck around for breakfast, Kisho. I won't force you, but it would mean a lot to us."

Kisho smiled and said, "That's fine with me. I won't be leaving for a few hours anyway. You get yourselves cleaned up. I'll be waiting."

Reina and Kisho shared a smile. Reina grabbed the pistol from the floor and said, "Nick, help your sister get to the bathroom. I'll be there in a minute. I just have to put this thing away. We don't need it."

Nick happily agreed to help his sister. The day proceeded as planned. Reina helped Julie bathe, then everyone else showered separately. They enjoyed a scrumptious breakfast at a local diner, then they said their goodbyes as Kisho departed.

During the weeks after the event, the Knight family relocated to a hotel with the money earned from their episode of Unearthly Happenings. Edmund was disappointed, but Rose convinced him to release the money. The partners agreed: it was for the greater good. Julie continued to see apparitions, but she never felt like she was in danger. She never saw her father again, either.

Kisho returned to Japan to aid a family and cleanse a hotel in Tokyo. The battle would last months while pushing him to his limits...

Join the mailing list!

Are you interested in more *unearthly happenings?* Are you a fan of dark, gruesome horror? If so, you should sign-up for my mailing list. I release dark, disturbing horror books every 28 days. Most of my books are grim and violent—I'm an extreme horror author after all—but I occasionally release supernatural horror novels like this one. By joining my mailing list, you'll be the first to know about new releases and deep discounts. Best of all, the process requires very little effort on your part and it's completely *free!* Oh, and you'll only receive 1-2 emails per month. Okay, you might receive three emails a month every now and then, but that's not common. You won't get any spam, either. Visit this link to sign-up: http://eepurl.com/bNl1CP

Dear Reader,

Hello! Thanks for reading *Her Suffering.* This book had a few disturbing scenes, but it was tame compared to my others. However, even though the book deals with ghostly entities, I understand that it also deals with sexual assault, which is an understandably sensitive subject. As you know, Julie is constantly attacked by her father's spirit. If this offended you, please accept my sincerest apologies. I write to entertain, terrify, and occasionally traumatize, but I don't write to *purposely* offend. I try my best not to be an obnoxious asshole.

Her Suffering was inspired by 1982's *The Entity*—the movie, not the book. To be attacked by an invisible intruder—an unidentified entity—I think that is a physically and psychologically terrifying concept. I tried to combine that idea from *The Entity* with the family-drama aspects of *The Exorcist.* I aimed to create a horrific experience for Reina and Julie, and I wanted Nick to be the one who sees it all from the sidelines. He's not directly affected and he's not allowed to help, so it places him in the most hopeless position.

I have been thinking about making this into a series of standalone novels that would either follow Kisho or Rose and Edmund or both parties. If I go down this path, I would try to release one book in the *Unearthly Happenings* series each year. And, you'd be able to read all of these books in any order. That's what's great about standalone novels. It's an idea I've been toying with for a long time. I plan on visiting the Akaska Weekly Mansion and other eerie locations sometime in the future to begin planning the next book. Or, I might even write a prequel that depicts Kisho's possession in the 1970s. Let me know what you think about that in an email or a review.

If you enjoyed this book, *please* leave a review on Amazon.com. Your review will help me improve on my writing, it will help me decide what to write next, and it will help other readers find this book. Good or bad, your reviews lead to better books. If you need help writing your review, here are some questions for you. Did you like the story? Did you connect with the characters? Do you enjoy my supernatural novels? Should I stick to extreme horror books? Would you like to see more books in the *Unearthly Happenings* series? Answering these questions will help me understand you, the reader.

You can also show *more* support by sharing this book. Post a link on Facebook or Twitter, share the cover on Instagram and Snapchat, write a post about it on your blog, send the paperback to a long-lost friend, or buy a Kindle copy for your neighbor. Sharing books is an excellent way to support independent authors and it's just great for society. People love good books, don't they?

I'm at an interesting point in my writing career. Again, I'm *still* not making 'Stephen King'-money, I am technically poor by most social standards, but my books are performing well by *my* standards—more of you are buying and reading every month. That means *you*, the reader, has been helping me a lot. I have shelter, internet, movies, books, and television. I don't live in a huge house, go on fancy vacations, or own a fleet of cars and boats, but I'm happy right now. I hope I can continue to entertain you and I hope you continue to support me. It means a lot to me. *Thank you.*

Finally, if you're a horror fan, feel free to visit my Amazon's Author page. I've published nearly two dozen horror novels, a few sci-fi/fantasy books, and some anthologies. Want to read a violent revenge thriller? Check out *Ms. Vengeance.* Looking for an extremely disturbing story about youth, love, and jealousy? Check out next month's book, *Our Dead Girlfriend.* If you're new to my books, feel free to check out some of my older novels, too. If you've already read my other books, you know the drill: I release a new book every month, so keep your eyes peeled. Once again, thank you for reading. Your readership keeps me going through the darkest times!

Until our next venture into the dark and disturbing,
Jon Athan

P.S. If you have questions (or insults), you can

contact me via Twitter @Jonny_Athan, or my Facebook page, or through my business email: info@jon-athan.com. If you're an aspiring author, I'm always happy to offer a helping hand. Even if you only have a simple question, don't hesitate to contact me. Thanks again!

Printed by Amazon Italia Logistica S.r.l.
Torrazza Piemonte (TO), Italy